A STRUGGLE OF THE HEART

By Marie Fostino

ACKNOWLEDGMENT

A young woman faces the age-old dilemma: what to do when you are torn between two lovers. Do you believe in love at first sight or should you get to know the person before you give your heart away. Do you have the intelligence to know your future or are the events- tragedies- happy times you experience shape your future. This book comes from my heart after becoming a paramedic when experiencing the Oklahoma Bombing and the different people I was fortunate enough to get to know who studied with me. A Struggle of the Heart by Marie Fostino

My heart goes out for the families who lost loved ones during this disaster. I also want to thank the firefighters, police, medical personal and volunteers who helped saving lives during this terrible time.

This book is dedicated to my husband, my five children and my nine grandchildren and for the patience and love that we have for each other during our adventure of life and for their patience as I wrote this book.

I also want to thank you, the readers, for taking the time to read what I have written. I hope you enjoy this book

Praise for A Struggle of the Heart

"A struggle of the heart is a beautiful read that makes you think about the choices that define your life and help make you the person you are meant to be. Fostino describes the characters in beautifully remarkable detail and draws you into their lives - making it seem as if you know them personally. The vivid description in this book captures the reader's attention and brings you into the story. A Struggle of the Heart is an emotional tale about finding one's self, the struggles of love, and the choices we make when it comes to both." ***Amazon Review, 5 Stars***

"A Struggle of the Heart is an emotional and enjoyable read. I enjoyed the historical reference to the events in Oklahoma because they helped to make the novel that much more relatable." ***Amazon Review, 4 Stars***

"This is a story of love and romance that is believable. Love lost, life changing events, passion, bewildering pain... three good people who all deserve a fairy tale ending that can only be possible for two. Who would you pick? At the end of the day, this story is a beautiful tribute to one of the Great American Tragedies."

Amazon Review, 5 stars

Table of Contents

Chapter 1

My First Love

"Are you all right?" I asked with some trepidation.

"No," he said and my heart constricted into a tense ball. Aaron planted his feet firmly on the bench. He leaned forward, placed his elbows on his knees and rested his head on his hands. I sat down next to him and after a few silent moments, slipped my arm tenderly around him. My heart skipped a beat as I wondered what could be so wrong when everything had seemed so right.

"I need to tell you something," he said finally "and I'm not sure you're going to like it."

My heart sank with those words and I managed to mumble, "Okay, go on."

"Do you know what ran through my mind before I came over to see you today?" Not waiting for an answer, he continued. "I thought about the way we met, our date fishing, and how funny you were trying to impress me with your skills."

I gazed up at him and gently squeezed his waist. "I thought about that too," I replied nervously, wondering where all this was leading.

"I remember everything about those first few days I spent with you," he said, his voice shaky. I felt a distinct trembling inside and wondered if Aaron was about to break up with me.

"My point is that I loved each and every moment we shared together, Annette and I did not expect anything like this to happen." He shoved a hand in his pocket and pulled out a rubber band to tie back his long black hair.

"What's going on, Aaron?" I asked in frustration.

"I didn't expect to fall in love," he said closing his eyes for a moment. I could feel hot tears gathering behind my eyes and blinked to stop them from falling down my cheeks.

"I love you too… so what's the problem?"

"I have to leave on Thursday for Fort Jackson in South Carolina. I'm going to boot camp, so our time together will soon be over."

Although I heard the words, I could not rationalize or accept what he said. We're in love! My mind screamed. How could he do this to me?

"I'm so sorry, Annette but I have to go," he said almost in a whisper. Aaron turned to me drawing me into his captivating dark eyes. Then he pulled me close and hugged me desperately, as if for the last time. I began to sob uncontrollably and he cradled me in his arms for some time. I had never been in love before and Aaron's shattering news tore at my heart. Even though we had only known each other for a brief time, I fell hard for him. This just could not be the end.

Chapter 2
Growing Up in Lawton

I first met Aaron in my early 20's while working at a beauty salon in Norman, Oklahoma. Although I never believed in love at first sight, we seemed to click instantly. Over only a matter of weeks, we shared a whirlwind romance and fell deeply in love. I could never have imagined meeting my first love when I moved from my hometown of Lawton about 65 miles away. I was born in that small town in 1974 and first learned hair styling at the local beauty salon where my mother worked.

Mom was a kind woman, short and pretty. She never met anyone as a stranger but all as friends. She always offered a friendly hello with a hug for everyone she met. Her favorite part of working at the salon she said, was styling the hair of little old ladies. She recalled a quote in the Bible that said a woman's hair was her *crown and glory.* She wanted these grannies to be able to gaze in the mirror and feel beautiful.

I loved when she brought me to work with her. I often watched her help these ladies get up from a chair under the dryer and walk to her station. She was so gentle with them as she took out their rollers and brushed their hair, and she listened intently when they talked about their families or what they planned to do for the rest of the day. After she finished their hair, she personally guided them to their cars and more hugs were shared. Before they left, her patrons always returned her kindness with huge smiles. Mom harbored a special place in her heart for these elderly women and I aspired to be just like her.

During the many hours I spent at the salon while growing up, I delighted in skimming through her hair styling books to find just the right look. The other beauticians treated me well, often practicing up dos on my hair or letting me play with theirs. I have to say, I had a great time playing beauty shop. As for mom, her hair was cut in layers and sat on top of her shoulders. Miss Clairol kept her color a rich dark brown. Many people said I looked just like her and I considered that a compliment.

My dad, on the other hand, was a short Italian man with a thick head of black hair and a big nose like Jimmy Durante. I think I got my long dark hair from him and most definitely his nose! Unlike my more outgoing mother, he was a quiet man who kept to himself and loved to cook. When he was young, he attended cooking school and held a part-time job at a restaurant. However, he hated his working hours because he got off at 2 a.m. and had to work every holiday. But he did like the kitchen atmosphere and spent much of his time preparing plates of appetizing food.

When the cooking school held the baking portion of the course, my dad quit and decided to take up baking instead. After he graduated, he secured a job at a large bakery and started on the day shift. He loved the hours but after a couple of years, he became supervisor and his hours changed. He would leave at 3 a.m. and not arrive home until after 5 p.m. Although he did not like those hours either, he knew baking and enjoyed the challenges

of the bakery whether the problem was too much yeast in the mix or the heat was too high in the ovens.

When I was young, dad took me on a tour of his own bakery. It was amazing to see the large bowls and huge mixers. The dough ran down a moving ramp to a room kept at a special temperature to allow it to rise. Then the ramp moved the dough to another area where it was kneaded and finally put into pans to raise again. The pans were then placed into large ovens and after they were baked, the bread was turned out on a clean ramp that took it to the packaging area. Sometimes he brought home freshly baked bread or sweet rolls that were just made that morning. What a treat!

My parents seemed to be completely opposite of each other. While dad was passive, a loner and happy to be by himself, mom was always busy doing something for someone else. She said God put us here to help others whenever the need arose. She hated to be alone and if it was too quiet, she turned on the radio or television for noise. I soon realized that I had a little of both my parents built into me. Although I loved to keep busy whether it was with a school project or spending time with my parents cooking in the kitchen, I also cherished the quietness of my room. I particularly liked to lay on my bed with the window open so I could hear the birds and read a good book in solitude.

Holidays were a big deal at our house but when dad worked on those days, we celebrated the day after. He explained that bakeries had to ensure there was plenty of bread the day after a holiday when everyone ran to the stores to restock food. On one Thanksgiving that fell on a

Thursday, mom and I baked apple pies and prepared what we could for our feast the following day. Meanwhile, we turned on the television to watch the Thanksgiving Day Parade. Then we settled in to watch a good movie like Casa Blanca and waited for Friday to arrive. That day, dad made spaghetti sauce while mom prepared a turkey. One thing we enjoyed doing together was cooking in the kitchen, so mom and dad took turns letting me help them. Our dinner usually consisted of turkey, stuffing and sweet potatoes with marshmallows on top, broccoli and cheese, and of course, dad's tasty and traditional Italian dish, spaghetti and meatballs.

Mom usually asked some of her elderly customers from the beauty salon that did not have family in town over to join us. A couple of ladies always accepted her invitation and brought sweet potato or pumpkin pie. The table was decorated in orange and brown colors with a flower arrangement on top and a couple of candles, which she lit for dinner. With good food, great friends and interesting conversation, we always savored our holiday dinner – even if it was a day late!

While growing up, my family spent many days at Mount Scott, which was part of the nearby Wichita Mountains. Other than the mountains, Lawton was primarily flat land with only a few trees. Sometimes while driving there, we were forced to stop and wait as families of Buffalo crossed the road. As well, hardly a visit went by without spotting long horned cattle or prairie dogs along the mountainside. When I was little, mom let me climb around the rocks as long as I did not

wander too far and watched out for snakes. I also scampered around a place called The Holy City in the Wichita Mountain Refuge, which resembled Israel during Biblical times. Every Easter, we returned to watch an Easter Passion Play held at the site and every year in May, we attended Arts for All Festival.

My best friend was Lynn Mahoney, who lived just a couple of houses away from me. We were the same height but she was Irish with short wavy brown hair, pale skin and a petite form. I, on the other hand, displayed my pure Italian heritage with my olive skin, long dark hair and of course, my over-sized nose. Lynn and I grew exceptionally close despite the fact that her family was wealthier than mine. I could always tell by the way she dressed in the newest fashions but she did not hold her nose in the air and this difference never got in the way of our friendship. My family was not rich but we were middle class and never hurt for anything.

Lynn's family and mine were also good friends and always looked out for each other. In fact, all the people who lived on our block got along well, so it was easy to maintain a tight knit neighborhood. Many a barbecue was held in our back yard sharing our food and swimming in our pool. Of course, being Italian my dad always brought out a big bowl of spaghetti to share as well. We also held block parties and played softball in the street, blocking it off to any oncoming cars.

Lynn and I attended the same high school, where I had a handful of friends. I did not follow the crowd and kept up my grades. I was not a straight 'A' student but my grades were above average. I always did my homework

and never got into trouble. Lynn and I often walked to school together, sometimes attended the same classes and shared all of our deepest secrets. After school, I attended all the football games with Lynn and my other girlfriends, and flirted with the players. I went on a few dates during those years but only when Lynn gave me permission since she kept up with the scoop on who was going out with whom. I guess my life was kind of boring in some respects but in my eyes, it was an exceptional one that I will always treasure.

As I grew older, I sometimes went on trips with the girls to Oklahoma City to take in its excellent shopping malls. The malls in Lawton were so small that you could walk from one end to the other in just a matter of minutes. They were not particularly busy either, which I figured had something to do with the army base in town. Most of the population extended from the base, which offered cheaper shopping.

Sometimes, we also went out to eat at a restaurant called Meers. The restaurant, which included a small post office, appeared rustic and antique. We chowed down on juicy and sumptuous burgers served with drinks in old canning jars. Outside the restaurant, I often saw an elderly Indian fellow with long dark gray hair in a ponytail sitting on the front porch. He sold snake skins, which some folks in those days believed held healing properties - a belief still held in some countries today. Interestingly, the Oklahoma Geological Survey installed a seismograph inside the restaurant in 1985 to monitor

what became known as the Meers vault - a crack in the earth's crust. Eventually, the site became an observatory.

By the time I was 16, it seemed a natural transition for me to follow in my mother's footstep as a beautician. Although she never said it, she often hinted that I should and during my senior year of high school, she got her way. I worked at the salon shampooing hair, sweeping the floor and washing towels. Although this job only offered a minimum wage, my customers seemed to appreciate my services. They seemed particularly fond of my head rubs because I took my time with their shampoo. In return, they often gave me a dollar tip.

Sometimes, the other beauticians helped me pick out a new haircut or style for myself. They even offered advice on such things as what color I should dye my hair that week or whether a few streaks of blond would suffice. As well, I relished in the gossip they shared about the latest upcoming movies or what the movie stars were doing in their more glamorous lives.

When I graduated high school, I went on to Beauty School following my mother's footsteps. During my days when I wasn't at school I would practice what I learned between giving shampoos at the beauty shop. When I graduated I got a job as a beautician at the shop. My mother was so proud.

At first, I needed a little help giving tints or frostings but I liked learning everything first hand from mom and the other beauticians at the shop. It was much more fun than being in school. Sometimes the other beauticians passed one of their younger customers on to me and I

enjoyed cutting the latest styles. Mom also taught me how to give perms and to this day, whenever I catch a whiff of that familiar scent, I think of her.

Chapter 3
Spreading My Wings

For my mother, being a beautician was quite satisfying but over time, I found that I needed more. Although I tried desperately to be like her, sadly, it was just not enough. I also felt stuck in Lawton, with no new young people for customers, except for the fellows from nearby Fort Sill and their wives. Boredom seemed to grip me in a tight hold and I realized that I needed to do something more challenging with my life.

Mom also harbored bigger dreams for me. She knew me better than anyone and probably sensed my discontent. She eventually told me that I should get a college education. In her day, she said, a high school education was enough to land a good job but times had changed. She wanted me to be able to take care of myself. Finally, she insisted that I attend college and kept after me to decide what I wanted to do. Her dream for me was to go to a Lawton college, acquire a degree in anything, get married and have a family.

I knew mom did not want me to leave town to further my education but I longed to experience a larger, more exciting city, especially after my best friend, Lynn moved to Norman after high school. She explained that the city was also comprised of flat land but had much more to offer. The city hosted a number of free festivals throughout the year including The Medieval Fair, Groove Fest Musical Festival and a Main Street Christmas Parade, just to name a few. The only drawback was that Norman lay within what was called

Tornado Alley, which meant a severe weather season that lasted from March through August.

Lynn said she was going to move into a dorm at the University of Oklahoma about 20 miles south of Norman so she could pursue her dream of becoming a lawyer. She was certainly smart enough and her family had the money but her mother did not want her to leave and tried to talk her into living on campus at Cameron University, here in Lawton. However, Lynn knew it was time to spread her wings. She felt it was her time to explore, see the world and grow up on her own. I know it broke her mother's heart because my mom talked with her on the phone for hours trying to console her. Lynn and I always kept in contact and her new experiences sounded so exiting. Perhaps, I could go there too, I thought.

After living on campus for a year, she decided to move off campus to rent a room in a house with some other college students. She called me to see if I was interested in moving there too. Just the thought of joining Lynn and the other college students was far too tempting. Lynn said it was time for me to take a chance - to see the world without my parents. It was time to go off on my own, she noted and I knew she was right. My dream was to further my education at the University of Oklahoma too, although I did not yet know what courses I would take.

I decided to make it my goal to work for a year or so until I gathered enough money to make the big move. The only problem was how to share my dream with mom. I definitely did not wish to break her heart. Being an only child, I naturally felt pangs of guilt over the thought of

leaving her. She had great difficulty getting pregnant and suffered a couple of miscarriages before I arrived. Mom always called me a miracle baby, which made breaking the news that much more difficult. She was also the type of woman who always did things for others. She said God put us here to help people who needed us. How could I tell this wonderful woman that I wanted to leave her?

It was the summer of 1994 when I finally summonsed the courage to tell her about my plan to join Lynn in Norman. We had made plans to spend the day at Mount Scott and I watched as she nimbly climbed the rocks ahead of me. Although she was 21 years older than me, she was still quite agile and adventurous. We continued to climb upward toward our favorite tree and I felt a distinct change in the air. No matter how warm the day might seem at first, it was always a little cooler and windier on the mountain.

"Come on slow poke," mom shouted as I scrambled to catch up with her.

"Mom," I said gently.

She turned to look at me for just a moment before she continued on. I offered a cheerful smile and faithfully follow her. The sight was always breathtaking on the mountain, especially on this day as dusk began to take over producing pink clouds in the baby blue sky. I caught up to her and as I reached her side, she put her arm around me.

"Beautiful, isn't it?" she whispers as if this was the first time she'd seen it. We stood in awe, lost in our own thoughts for a brief moment before the right time came to speak.

"Mom," I said still admiring at the sky. "I made a decision." Her hand never left my arm while she stood in silence surveying the scene below. "I plan to move in with Lynn and go to college in Norman."

Mom sighed aloud but it seemed as though she already knew what I was going to say. Then she turned and hugged me close for a moment.

"Come on, sweetie," she said letting her eyes study my face. "We should hike back to the car before it gets too dark."

She kissed me softly on the cheek before letting me go and we began our trek back. During the drive home, mom still did not respond to my news. Perhaps she saw my restlessness and figured out that I would want to do this. Maybe, she had already talked to Lynn's mom. On the other hand, she might have hoped I would change my mind. Either way, she did not try to talk me out of it or say anything negative about my plans. In fact, she did not broach the subject until the following morning.

"So you've decided to go on to college," she noted, pausing for a moment as she hustled around the kitchen. "What do you want to major in?" she asked sincerely.

"I don't know yet." I poured myself a cup of coffee and sat down. I really had not decided. Lynn wanted to be a lawyer and she had the brains to keep up with those studies. All I knew at that point was that I needed my prerequisites first and by the time I had them, I figured I would know which direction I wanted to take with my life. Lynn said a lot of students who attended college did not know what they wanted. I could not wait to talk to a

counselor and set up some kind of plan but for the time being, it was difficult enough just letting mom know that I planned to leave home.

"Well, you're certainly old enough to decide what you want out of life" she said, "and I would never keep you from it."

I did not realize that my body tensed until she said that and a loud sigh escaped my lips. I ran up to her with my arms open wide and squeezed her lovingly.

"Thank you!" I squealed over and over again. "Thank you!" I could not help noticing tears in her eyes but she quickly wiped them away saying a fly flew by her face.

"When do you plan to leave?" she asked when I finally let her go. We both moved to the kitchen table and sat down.

"I think I can save enough money for the spring semester," I said before taking a gulp of coffee. "So I will leave in January."

"Good," she said, a small smile forming at the edges of her mouth. "At least you'll still be here for Christmas. I think Lynn's mom said she would be here for the holidays too. Perhaps you two could drive back together?"

"What a great idea," I thought since it would be a couple of hours drive and it would not be so lonely if I had someone with whom I could car pool. I could not believe how understanding mom was about the whole thing. She had no idea how difficult it was to gather the courage to tell her.

Chapter 4
A New Life

By January 1995, I saved enough money to pay for the first semester of college. I figured that if I acquired a job at a beauty salon in Norman, I could save even more so I could come up with the necessary funds for the next semester and so on. At least, I had to try. During the next six months, I worked overtime taking on more customers and socking away as much as I could. In an effort to help, mom sometimes gave me an elderly customer of hers so I could earn a few extra dollars. I felt like I knew those ladies all my life both at the salon and at my house during holidays. They were most kind to me, often offering a little extra in tips.

Mom told my father about my plans and he immediately began taking care of my car. He told me he wished he had listened to his father when he tried to explain about changing the oil but dad was not into things like that. He paid to have the oil changed in my car; bought four new tires and had someone check out the engine.

Both of my parents seemed to take great pains to cram a lifetime into my last six months at home. I particularly treasured the dinners we prepared together so I could learn more about cooking. It would be something I needed to do for myself once I moved. As well, my parents always made sure they were around, talking to me all the time and just letting me know they were there for me.

They even helped calm my mind and nerves during the few times I got cold feet about my decision. After all, I did go to school to become a beautician and I was afraid I was letting my mother down. I remembered how proud she looked when I showed her my license. She could not wait to show her boss at the beauty salon and I got a station right next to hers. I could only imagine how hard it must be for a parent to let his or her only child leave home. However, mom and dad both let me know they supported me, were proud of me and trusted me.

I talked to Lynn and finally our plans were set. She would fly into Lawton and drive back with me right after New Years. Mom had Christmas at our house with Lynn's family over for dinner along with her sister, husband and their children. Of course, a few of her customers arrived to enjoy the festivities as well.

The holidays flew by so fast and before I knew it, it was time to say goodbye. After a few tears and many hugs, plus sack lunches mom made for Lynn and I, we took off. How accelerating to begin this new adventure. The weather was cold with snow falling but I stayed warm in the car with so much enthusiasm running through my veins.

We finally arrived at a two-story house with a built-in garage. I could hear the sound of conversation as Lynn opened the front door. Once inside, she introduced me to her roommates, Jim, Zack and Jessica. I was then shown to my room where I proceeded to settle in. After supper, we all sat down and got to know each other.

Jim, who had big brown eyes and brown hair that swept over his ears, reminded me of the Beatles from the

60's. He said he loved to play his guitar, and hoped to be a rock and roll star one day. To that end, he decided to attend school and major in music. He told me that it was much harder than he thought it would be. He still needed to acquire his prerequisites in English, math and science, along with music theory, music history and learning to play the keyboard.

Zack, who seemed to be a wiz at math, wanted to become an accountant. Unlike Jim, his personality seemed low key and quiet. Surveying his tight haircut and skinny body, he did resemble somewhat of a geek. Jessica, who seemed somewhat conceited, was tall with long straight hair and looked like a model. She explained that she was taking business classes but hoped that in time she could travel to California, attend acting school and become a movie star. For the time being, however, she was content as a student at the University of Oklahoma.

The house we shared was ideal for college students since it came furnished with couches and chairs, beds, dressers and kitchen utensils, all stored and waiting to be used. With five bedrooms, it was decorated in earth tones with carpeting in the living room and tile on the kitchen floor. The upstairs had four bedrooms with a shared bathroom between them. I was lucky enough to get the room downstairs, which was a lot smaller than the others but I did not have to share a bathroom with anyone. This situation had its drawbacks however, because the living room and kitchen with all their noises were so close to my room. I decided to purchase a box fan, just for the

humming noise to drown out the noise from the television or anyone who decided to stay up late to party.

I found a job after only a few days as a hair stylist at Unisex Beauty Salon. The salon was located in a little strip mall that included a grocery store, a couple of restaurants and a small post office. The windows were covered with sheer white curtains and the front door was glass with no covering. Walking in the front door, patrons were greeted at the appointment desk. To the right of the desk sat a little end table with some hair styling books and a few chairs around to sit and wait for one's turn. Along the wall on the opposite side, six stations were lined up with dryers and in the back were the shampoo bowls. It was a cute little place and I was certainly thrilled to have a job.

I decided to wait one more semester before I started school. That way, I could save more money and would know the area a lot better by then as well. My plan was to start school the following summer.

The first week at work unfortunately seemed pretty slow. Being a beautician was not the easiest way to earn a living. In Lawton, the cost of a permanent was $30 but in Norman, people paid as much as $60. Even though I could potentially make more money, I needed to have customer first.

January flew by and slowly more people walked into the salon requesting haircuts with a perm or a hair color thrown in. It was a good thing that I had not started school yet because I was using some of the money I saved for school to live on.

Chapter 5
An Unexpected Customer

One day while relaxing and reading a novel between customers on my hairstyling chair, a young man walked in. I did not look up because it was not my turn yet for a new customer. All of the hairdressers rotated the new people and the girl beside me was up next but this fellow walked right past her chair and stopped directly in front of mine.

"Ehem," he said to capture my attention. "Where's Suzie?"

Startled I peered up from my book and saw him staring right at me.

"You're sitting in her chair," he continued, his long black hair falling well below the collar of a tight shirt that accentuated his ample muscles. At first, I shrugged my shoulders without saying a word. Then I caught a smile forming on his face and adorable dimples appeared.

"I'm sorry," I replied quickly put down my book. "I work at this station now."

He still would not leave my station and I really needed the money, so I asked him what he wanted done.

"Will Suzie be back soon?" he asked ignoring my question.

I guess I could have asked the other girls who Suzie was and where she worked now but I chose not to do it. I felt an unusual stirring inside when this fellow looked at me. I had dates in high school but no one special and definitely no one who made me feel that way. It was

something so strong and so real that when he gazed into my eyes, I could not look away.

"I'd be glad to help you," I responded. "What did you say your name was?"

I guess I seemed a little rude asking him for his name and stealing a customer from Suzie. However, I did not believe she worked at the salon anymore since I had not met her during the entire month I worked there. Of course, it also had plenty to do with his smile – and those dimples!

He followed me to the sink and sat in the chair as if he had done this a thousand times before.

"Aaron Mohanti," he replied while lifting his hair to let me place a towel and cape around his neck.

Carefully, he laid his head in the sink and closed his eyes so he could enjoy the shampoo I was about to give him. It took a minute for the water to warm up before I let it spray on his scalp and then ran my fingers through his hair. Next I poured on some shampoo and massaged his head. I faintly overheard the gossip of the girls around me but was afraid to look up. They were saying something about this customer being Suzie's regular and how upset she would be if she knew he was not told where she was working. Then it was mentioned that it was really her own fault for not calling him and telling him that she had moved to another salon. I finished the shampoo and rinsed his hair. When done, I carefully folded the towel around his head and helped him sit back up.

"Good shampoo," he said as he followed me back to my station.

To the right of my chair, a stylist named Veronica was bleaching a woman's hair while she listened to her customer complain that her husband was cheating on her. She cried as she told Veronica that she saw the two of them at a restaurant one night when her husband said he had to work late. The smell of the bleach on the woman was so strong that it made my eyes water too.

To the left of my chair, Betty was fixing the hair of a nervous bride who wanted an up do. She came in to figure out what style she wanted on her wedding day, which was still two weeks away. From the corner of my eye, I noticed the owner, Carol, sitting at the front desk speaking on the telephone.

"I'm Annette Ferrari," I said, as Aaron got comfortable in my chair.

I held out my hand and that dimpled smile grew on his face again. He took my hand and shook it gently sending shivers down my body.

"Well, how can I help you today?" I asked attempting to ignore the sensation. I pulled out a comb to run it through his beautiful, jet-black hair that fell down between his shoulder blades. I was amazed that the comb went through so easily without many tangles and I hoped that he did not plan to have his gorgeous hair cut too short.

"I just need a trim," Aaron noted with a grin and I let out a sigh of relief.

"Are you new around here?" he asked keeping his chin down while I carefully trimmed around his neck. "I haven't seen you here before."

"Yes, I am," I answered. "I want to go to the University of Oklahoma and am trying to save up some more money to pay for my schooling."

He shook his head up and down as if he understood.

"Don't move your head unless you want short hair," I advised playfully.

"Oops, sorry. I sure hope you know how to use those scissors?" he quipped back. "I try to get a trim every six weeks but it looks like my regular girl isn't here anymore. Looking up at me he smiled and added, "Maybe, just maybe, you can be my new girl."

I couldn't help smiling back. I needed a few more steady customers and it would definitely be nice to see this fellow again. I remained quiet as I pinned up his hair preparing to cut it. I heard the girls around me gossiping quietly amongst themselves and with their customers. The one thing I loved about working in the beauty salon was the freedom to talk, gossip or even sing, if the mood struck. The radio was on and every once in a while, the phone rang.

"Where are you from?" Aaron asked finally.

"Lawton."

"Lawton. Not too far from home then. Isn't that home to Fort Sill?"

"Yes it is. It's a small army town but there's not a whole lot to do there." I did not know why I offered that information and felt a little embarrassed. I finished that

layer of hair and brought down more to cut letting him raise his head.

"Explain," Aaron said suddenly.

He caught me off guard because it seemed that he was actually interested. I slid the comb down his hair in between my fingers and lopped off another piece.

"Lawton is such a boring town. I really wanted to move to a bigger, more interesting city." My mind wandered back to my mom insisting that I go to college and keeping after me to decide what I wanted to do with my life. I felt stuck in Lawton and desperately needed to get out to explore other places.

"Do you like cutting hair?" he asked bringing me back to reality.

What a strange question, I thought. Why would I be here if I didn't? "Yes, I like styling hair," I replied firmly. "So tell me about you."

Aaron glanced at me in surprise as if he was unaccustomed to anyone showing interest in him too. To be honest, it felt rather odd to me as well to be talking so openly with a complete stranger.

"My parents are from the Wichita tribe and grew up on the reservation in Shawnee," he explained. "I attended a private school and went on to college for a couple of semesters until my mother got sick… but now I'm not so sure about that. I'm considering joining the army."

I glance at his face in the mirror and he looked up again, studying me for my response.

"I know," he remarked. "Why would I join the military instead of finishing school?"

I did not respond and waited for him to explain.

"First, the army pays for your schooling. You said yourself that you were working to pay for college."

"That's true."

"So why not? I can sign up for eight years, get my college paid for and go on with my life," he stated with a smug smile. I had the distinct impression that he was still trying to convince himself of the validity of his decision.

"You have it all planned out then?" I asked. I could not help feeling a tad jealous. I went to school to become a beautician and sure it was good for my mom but I realized that I still missed something. It was not what I wanted as a career. And although I made the move to Norman, I still did not know what I wanted to pursue. The man in my chair seemed to have his future all worked out.

I finally took his hair out of the clips and laid it around his shoulders. Then I turned the chair so he had to face me. Swiping some hair out of my face, I truly wished that I had it all together like he did. I could feel his eyes trace my face as I measured the hair by his shoulders making sure it was even.

"How old are you?" he asked.

"Don't you know you never ask a woman her age?" I quipped. Aaron smiled and looked slightly embarrassed.

"It's all right," I continued nonchalantly. "I'm 21… and you?"

"I'm 23. Do you have any brothers or sisters?" It suddenly seemed quieter than normal in the beauty salon as if everyone else was listening.

"No. I'm an only child - just my folks and me. My parents still live in Lawton and happy as clams after twenty-four years of marriage. Your turn," I challenged. Our eyes met and I could not look away.

"I'm also an only child but my mother passed away a year ago," he explained, a sad tone clear in his voice. "It has been difficult dealing with her death and seeing my father so upset. Maybe that's why I want to join the army. I need to get away and make something of myself... something that would make my dad proud."

I swallow hard, feeling a sudden dryness in my throat. I took a sip of the water from a glass at my station.

"I bet your dad is already proud of you," I said hoping to convey encouragement.

"I hope so."

"You don't sound too sure of yourself."

"Ever since mom died, he really hasn't been there for me, you know. He doesn't talk about her or anything for that matter, like he is all alone in this world."

"He doesn't have to say the words I am proud of you," I suggested. "Maybe he does it in other ways."

Aaron seemed to fall deep in thought, as I finish combing his hair.

"Well, what do you think?" I asked taking a hand mirror off the station and passing it to him. I turned his chair around so he could see the back of his head.

"Good job," he said giving only a quick glance at the mirror and keeping his eyes on me. I took off the cape and towel, and placed it on my station.

"That will be $16, sir."

He stood up, pulled a fifty out of his wallet and placed it in my hand. His hand wrapped around mine squeezing the money inside – again rousing feelings I'd never had before.

"No change," he whispered, his eyes focused on mine. I panicked.

"I can't take that big of a tip!" I said, my voice crackling.

"Will you let me take you out for lunch instead?" Aaron asked with a genuine smile.

"I don't have any customers for the next hour," I responded feeling suddenly lighthearted.

I had enjoyed the conversation with Aaron so far, so why not? He paid for his haircut and I let the girls know I would be back soon before following him out the door. I could sense the awkward stares on my back as I left the salon. I figured the other hairdressers knew something was up.

Chapter 6
Getting to Know Aaron

Aaron and I walked down the street to a little sandwich shop where he opened the door like a gentleman and let me pass inside first. The smell of the deli poured through the open door along with the noise of customers sitting at tables and those in line ordering food. I figured the food must be palatable since so many people had crowded into the small place.

"Have you ever eaten the sandwiches here?" he asked as we got in line. "I'm friends with the owner and it's really good."

"No," I replied.

A quant little place, the deli had a soda fountain on one side and only a few tables to sit at with red and black checkered table clothes. Fresh salami hung from the ceiling along with some sausage. The glass covered counter in front of us displayed various meats and cheeses. There were also different kinds of salads and noodles to choose from as side dishes. A middle-aged, heavy-set woman behind the counter offered the sweetest smile as we moved up to give her our order.

"Are you hungry?" Aaron asked.

"Actually, I am starved."

"Aaron!" said the woman obviously happy to see him. "How is your dad these days? Good to see you." Her voice sounded so kind and her eyes twinkled.

"He's okay," he replied obviously not wanting to go into detail. "Good to see you too, Thelma." Aaron scanned the meats and cheeses through the glass.

"I think I'll have the regular."

"Of course you will," Thelma said with a laugh, "and what about your friend?"

Her eyes shot up to me smiling and I noticed a few lines around them, as well as some grey hair at her temples. She actually made me feel at home.

"The same please."

"I like to see a girl who eats," Thelma said laughing even louder.

Her comment left me wondering just how much food I would actually get. I guess because I was slim, she thought I might be on a diet. We watched her make our sandwiches taking the salami roll and slicing it in front us, along with ham and pastrami. My mouth watered at the thought of the treat I was about to enjoy. Aaron paid for our meal and found us a seat at the only unoccupied table. He handed me my plate and sat across from me. We took a few bites in silence listening to the sounds of laugher and gossip in the background. More people materialized, as the line at the counter never seemed to shrink.

"So you come here all the time?" I asked.

"Well, I sort of grew up with these people. They were good friends with my mom and dad but when mom passed away, dad quit coming around to see anyone."

I sensed the deep sorrow in his voice again and felt the need to change the subject.

"So what are you doing with your time now? Are you going to school?"

"I was going to school before I decided to join the army. I talked to a recruiter and he asked me to make

sure this was the right decision for me so I decided to take the semester off."

"What kinds of questions did he ask you?" I enquired between bites truly enjoying my sandwich.

"First, he asked why I wanted to join?"

"Well?"

Aaron seemed to search for the right answer.

"Education, personal satisfaction… and pride," he replied with a laugh.

"What else did he ask you?"

"Well, there are many different jobs in the military. There are the guards, the reserves, enlisted men and officers. He explained what they were all about and said I should be certain to pick the right one. And aside from the army, there is also the navy, marines and air force to choose from… but he was an army recruiter so naturally he pushed that."

"Do you have anything in mind yet?" I asked wanting to know more. I noticed some people leaving nearby tables but they were quickly occupied again as we continue to talk.

"I like to shoot," Aaron noted. "I learned from my father and I'm pretty good with a rifle so I think I would like field artillery."

I shook my head in acknowledgment, my long hair sweeping across my shoulders. I swiped a stray strand behind my ear.

"I also love the outdoors," he continued. "I'm a good hunter and I really love to fish."

I smiled as I took another bite. It became quiet again between us as we continued to eat and let our minds lapse

into our own thoughts. Mine went back to my younger days when I went fishing with my dad. Fishing was his favorite pastime and I think he was somewhat disappointed that he did not have a son with whom to share this hobby. All the same, I did my best to enjoy it with him.

"A penny for your thoughts?" Aaron asked interrupting my daydream.

"Oh, I was back in time fishing with my dad," I said.

"You should have seen us," I said, my face feeling warm. "We were a pair, sneaking onto someone else's land, being quiet and hoping to catch the big one."

I caught myself laughing aloud and felt embarrassed again but Aaron's smile was so kind as he attempted to share my enthusiasm. I wondered what he is thinking. I knew little about him but realized that what I had learned so far, I liked. He seemed gentle, quiet and not at all pushy. When I finished my sandwich, I quickly looked at my watch and ran my fingers through my hair. Where did the time go? I wondered.

"I really have to get back to work," I announced wishing I could stay to talk more with this man.

Our conversation seemed so easy and natural. Aaron took my plate along with his to throw them in a nearby trashcan. As we reach the door, the lady behind the counter yelled over to us.

"Don't be strangers."

Aaron smiled and threw a kiss to her as we headed out. We walked side-by-side - close but not touching. When we reached the beauty salon, I turned to look up at him. His smile… and his dimples… were enchanting.

"Thanks so much for lunch," I said stretching out my hand. Aaron took it in his and gave a gentle squeeze.

"Can I see you again?" his eyes pleaded with me.

"Of course. I would like that very much." I searched my purse for a pen and paper to write down my telephone number. Afterward, I really hoped I did not appear too eager.

On Sunday morning, I heard a knock at my bedroom door. The sun pouring into the room let me know it would be a pleasant day.

"Annette, you up?"

I recognized the voice in my sleep. Pulling the covers up over my head, I ignored the sound, thinking I might still be dreaming.

"Annette, you have a phone call," Lynn giggled from the other side of my door.

Who would be calling me early in the morning on a Sunday? I wondered.

Suddenly, I sat up thinking it might be mom and something was wrong at home. Pulling my legs out of bed, I grabbed my robe. In the living room, Lynn and Jessica were watching television. With a hasty wave, I made my way to the kitchen where I found the phone on the counter.

"Hello… mom? Is everything all right?"

For a few seconds, there was dead silence and then I heard a male voice clearing his throat.

"Annette… good morning. Did I wake you?"

Although taken aback, I welcomed the familiar voice.

"Good morning, Aaron," I said in my squeaking morning voice.

"How are you today?"

"I'm not sure yet," I giggled. "I just got up."

"Oh, sorry about that."

"It's okay," I replied to put him at ease.

"Do you have any plans for today?"

"Not really. Well, except for going to church this morning."

I sat on the chair next to the counter and played with the long telephone cord wrapping it around my arm. As a child, I was baptized and my family always believed in going to church On Sunday. I truly enjoyed church and particularly liked to start each week that way. I believed in God and in prayer, and loved to hear a good sermon. Our church was rather small so everyone knew each other. In fact, Lynn's family usually sat with us, and Lynn and I would sometimes write notes to each other during the services.

"Well, I was thinking about going fishing or I could show you how to shoot a gun?" Aaron offered.

"Are you asking me out?" I teased.

"Yeah, I am," he replied confidently.

There was silence for a moment as he waited for my answer.

"You want to come to church with me first?" I asked.

"To church?"

"Yeah, to church," I repeated. "Don't you go?"

Aaron grew quiet but I could hear his breathing in a rhythmic beat.

"Not really," he admitted. "I used to go as a kid and even as an adult with my mom sometimes but after she got sick and died, I gave up on church."

I stretched my legs and arched my back trying to wake up as I listened.

"I'm so sorry to hear that," I responded in a sympathetic tone. "I want to go to church first so you can either go with me or wait for me and then we can go out."

Lynn and Jessica were listening to my conversation and shaking their heads as if to say, "No." Lynn then whispered, "Go out with him, silly." I kept waving my hand at them to stop.

"What time is church?" he asked sounding as if he did not want to disappoint me.

"Well, there are two services," I explained. "One at Ten a.m. and another at noon."

"Fine, I'll pick you up for the 10 o'clock service."

As I hung up the phone, I felt so happy that he decided to join me but the girls began yelling at me.

"What if he didn't want to go with you? What if he decided against taking you out?"

Jessica threw a pillow at me but I ignored both of them and quickly ran back to my room. I showered and dressed, and at 9:45 a.m. the doorbell rang. Aaron appeared dressed in khakis and a pressed shirt with a tie. His hair was combed neatly back into a ponytail. I wore a flowery orange and white dress with matching orange shoes. I let my hair fall freely down my shoulders.

Jim and Zack finally got up and sat in the living room in shorts and T-shirts. When Aaron walked in, I introduce him to them. They exchanged handshakes and

pleasantries before Lynn and Jessica came down the stairs in their Sunday best.

"Can we bum a ride with you two to church?" Lynn asked wearing a short skirt and form-fitting blouse.

I could see she was checking out Aaron as she spoke.

"Hi, I'm Lynn," she said extending her hand.

Aaron cordially shook hands with her and she smiled broadly.

"This is Jessica," she continued and Jessica shook hands with him as well.

"Nice to meet you," he replied looking somewhat confused.

I'm sure he thought it would only be the two of us as we all hopped into his car. I hoped we did not scare Aaron off but once we arrived at the church, he seemed to enjoy the service. I sat next to Aaron, while Jessica and Lynn sat next to me looking a little disappointed. The pastor spoke low-key and the music stayed in style with today's latest religious hit songs. Aaron did not sing the hymns but seemed to stay focused on the scripture message. After we prayed, I noticed out of the corner of my eye that he performed the sign of the cross and took out a chain from around his neck. He then kissed the emblem that hung from it.

By the time we got back to the house, the boys had made some sandwiches and were sitting in front of the television watching a football game – both with a can of beer in their hands. Aaron had brought some casual clothes to change into and used the upstairs bathroom

while I went to my bedroom to change. Before I left my room, Aaron had already returned downstairs.

"Help yourself," said Zack gesturing. "We made a lot of sandwiches. We plan to watch the games all day today and eat." Zack picked up another sandwich for himself and walked toward the fridge.

"Want to join us?" he asked as he withdrew another beer and made his way back to the living room couch.

"No thanks. I want to take Annette into the wilderness and see what she's made of."

"She used to go fishing as a kid," laughed Jim letting his eyes escape the television for a moment. "She sure has some funny stories to tell."

"Hey," I piped in as I came out of my room. I had on a pair of jeans and a tucked in T-shirt. Aaron was also in jeans with a tight polo shirt that accentuated his muscular chest and arms.

"Why don't the two of you have a sandwich before you venture out into the wilderness?" Jim suggested.

"Great. I'm starved," I said entering the kitchen. "Did you grab one?" I asked glancing up at Aaron. For a moment, he stood as still as a statue with his eyes glued to me.

"Not yet," he finally said.

"Well, dig in. I hate to eat alone."

As we stood in the kitchen and ate, we watched the boys whooping and hollering over the game. I went to the fridge to fetch us each a soda and again felt Aaron gawking. I must have had an amused look on my face as I set the cans on the counter.

"After this are we going out?" I asked.

"Yep. I thought we'd go to the reservation and either do some fishing or I could teach you how to shoot."

I scrunched up my nose at the thought of holding a gun. Lynn and Jessica stepped into the kitchen talking rather loudly, as if we were not even there. It seemed like an ill attempt to garner Aaron's attention but it did not work. Looking dejected, they each grabbed a sandwich and went back to their conversation. Aaron and I finished ours and thanked the boys for sharing with us.

Once outside, Aaron opened the car door for me. It was February and one thing I knew about Oklahoma was that the weather could change drastically in just 24 hours. I remembered times when it snowed when I was growing up. Mom would take me outside to make a snowman. We often did this quickly because the next day, it could be 50 degrees. Of course, the snow and the snowman would melt. This day, the weather seemed unusually warm. It was in the 60's and I was wearing a jacket but brought a pair of gloves and a hat just in case it suddenly cooled off.

Chapter 7
Our First Date

"Did you say we're going to the reservation?" I asked as Aaron put his foot on the gas pedal and we drive off.

He smiled and turned on the radio. After finding the station he wanted, he answers me.

"Yeah, I heard that you like to fish," he said amused, "so I think we should find out how good you are?"

His eyes never left the road as he pointed toward the back seat. There he had set some fishing rods, a tackle box and two pairs of old army pants with suspenders as well as boots to fit over our shoes. I smiled and giggled under my breath.

"What if I said I wanted to learn how to shoot?" I challenged.

"I have a rifle in the trunk, if that's what you'd prefer," he said flashing a smile.

"No thanks," I conceded.

I kept quiet for a moment as I gathered my thoughts. At the same time, the tune on the radio seemed to grow louder.

"You don't mind, do you?" he asked almost alarmingly.

"No, of course not."

We drove in silence for the next ten minutes just listening to the radio.

"How long is the drive going to be?" I asked anxiously.

"It's about an hour to Shawnee and a little longer to the lake."

I felt like an annoying child asking, "Are we there yet?"

"Tell me about some of your fishing expeditions with your father," Aaron urged.

"Well, dad's idea of fishing was to drive until he found a lot of trees covering a hill," I explained. "He was pretty sure he'd find a pond behind them but unfortunately, it was usually on someone else's private land."

Aaron laughed as he continued to drive.

"Then dad parked the car, grabbed the tackle box and fishing gear, and we walked past the trees and climbed over a fence to the pond. He'd put liver on my hook instead of a worm and throw the line out into the water. He told me to stand quietly so I wouldn't scare the fish so I waited with the pole in my hand anticipating when the bobber would sink. It was always a thrill when the bobber sank and my dad helped me reel in whatever jiggled on the hook."

"You used liver? What about worms?"

"I used to be afraid of worms?" I confessed. "Anyway, dad said liver worked better."

"Really? You were afraid of itty bitty worms?" Aaron teased.

"Yeah, but I'm not anymore," I replied folding my arms obstinately across my chest.

"Well, we'll see," he replied needling me even more.

I decided right then and there to show him that I could do anything a man could do – what he could do. I was not the dainty little girl he imagined and I would prove it. Aaron noticed my body tense.

"Hey, I didn't mean to upset you," he said offering a dimpled grin.

How could I ever stay mad at him!

"What did you usually catch," Aaron asked glancing over at me.

"Bass and sometimes small ones. When that happened, dad took the little rascal off and threw it back into the water. Other times, there was nothing on the hook - not even the liver. Somehow those fish were smart enough to eat the food and not get caught!" I laughed.

"Did you ever catch any of those big ones?" Aaron asked glancing over at me.

I wondered for a moment if he was really interested in me or just wanted to talk about fishing.

"No, not really unless you count the boot I reeled in once," I joked. "Of course, I was disappointed but he put fresh bait on the hook and I tried again. Dad said I needed to be patient - the fish would come."

"I can just picture you with your dad. I see you running around the water's edge in pigtails with farmer's pants on and wearing a pink, ruffled blouse," he smiled. "Your dad likely told you not to get too close or you might fall in."

"Well, dad said fishing was a time to be quiet, to reflect on and enjoy nature. He insisted that I not talk, which I have to admit, was pretty hard."

At that moment, I wondered what a weird way it would be to spend a first date, if Aaron felt the same. I would much rather spend our time in conversation so I could learn more about him.

"Go on," he urged.

"Well, we were so quiet that I could hear the flies circling around the bait and the birds chirping in the trees. Dad looked so peaceful holding his rod, as if he was deep in thought. I would find a big rock to sit on as my line floated in the water and my reflection peered back up to me. Once I screamed because I noticed a snake swimming in the water. I startled my dad so badly that it made him jump which in turn caused him to drop his rod in the pond. He sure wasn't happy about that!"

Aaron broke out laughing again.

"And if that wasn't enough, when we walked back to our car we realized that someone left a nasty note on the windshield telling us they never wanted to see us on their land fishing again. Our next surprise were the holes in the tires of his car from a gun. Someone was really mad!"

Aaron laughed hysterically, as I continued.

"We had to walk a long time before we found a telephone to call mom to come and rescue us. When she arrived, she actually said that this type of incident was long overdue and that dad should know better than fish on private property. In reply, dad just grumbled under his breath but that was the last time he took me fishing."

"Wow," said Aaron. "You two had quite the adventures."

"Yes, I guess we did. Fishing was one thing that dad and I could share together."

"Did you learn how to clean the fish?" Aaron asked.

"Ew! You mean actually hold a dead fish and gut it?"

"Yes, that's what I mean," he replied letting out a hearty laugh.

"No, I never did that."

"Well, maybe you'll learn how today."

"No way!" I replied. "I'm not touching them!

"Aw, come on. You just might like it."

"Ah, I really don't think so." I paused for a moment, not to consider that idea but to wonder how Aaron could ever coax me to do something like that.

"You know, my dad used to go fishing with his dad too," I said hoping to redirect the conversation.

"Really?"

"In fact, sometimes the three of us would go fishing together. Unlike dad though, grandpa never trespassed and did not expect me to be quiet all the time. He would take me to the other side of the pond away from dad where we could talk and laugh. He even let me throw in my line and reel it back in over and over again just for fun."

"It sounds like you loved your grandpa very much."

"Yeah, I sure did. Grandpa was a quiet and simple man, always kind and very attentive toward me. He often came over to our house when I was young. I really enjoyed the stories he told me of when he was growing up and his experiences during the war."

"He went to war?" Aaron asked, his interest perking up.

"Well, he never finished high school because he joined the army when he was 18. He fought in the infantry in World War II and learned to drive a truck. When his time was

up, he got a job as a truck driver. At that time, he manually loaded big boxes onto his truck and then by hand, took the goods into the stores where he delivered them. Dad told me that in high school, he got a job at the warehouse where grandpa worked and also loaded the trucks but he decided that he didn't want to do manual labor for a living."

"I can understand that," Aaron interceded.

"Grandpa also liked to tinker with things around the house, including ours. He knew a lot about carpentry and electricity so when our family moved into another house and found that the porch was falling down, grandpa got the tools he needed and rebuilt it. He also installed the paneling in our hallway and put new cabinets in the kitchen."

"He sounds like a great man to have around. Is he still alive?"

"Sadly, no."

"How long did he live?"

"Not long enough as far as I'm concerned. It was a painful experience when we realized that he was becoming forgetful. My parents took him to a doctor and learned that he suffered from early Alzheimer's disease. They moved him into our home and at first we thought the doctors were wrong. However, grandpa soon forgot where the bathroom was or how to make a cup of coffee. Dad sometimes got mad at him for not remembering something so easy but mom was much more compassionate. She would put her arm around him and help him with whatever he needed."

"Alzheimer's is a terrible disease," Aaron noted.

"Yes, it is. For my grandpa, it exacerbated quickly and he soon had the mind of a child. When he became more confused, I spent time reading to him. I hoped that in some way, it might help his ability to think. We also went through the photo albums and I pointed out who was in the pictures. Grandpa died in his room when I was just 12 years old."

"You obviously still miss him."

"I sure do. He was an amazing man."

I found myself talking so freely with Aaron, which was quite unusual since we really did not know each other yet.

"Well, it's wonderful that you have some good memories with your grandfather," he said. "Today, let's see how much you learned fishing with him and your dad."

"I've been talking for quite a while," I noted. "Tell me more about you."

"What do you want to know?"

"Well, do you have a job?" I blurted out without thinking. I figured he knew what I did for a living so I should know too.

"Not at the moment" he paused looking a little uncomfortable. "I told you that I talked with a recruiter. Well, let me back track first."

He sighed aloud leaving me with the impression that he was reluctant to be so honest with me yet.

"I went to college for a year full time and took 16 credit hours each semester," he explained. "My mom had to go to the hospital for a hernia, which was totally unexpected. Her name was Martha by the way. Just a

hernia, you say?" He shrugged his shoulder. "Should be nothing, right? Well, the hernia ruptured so they put some sort of mesh over her abdomen wall to help with the new growth after they repaired it. The mesh acted as scaffolding for the new growth of her tissue, which eventually incorporated the mesh into the surrounding area. Well, the mesh became infected and my mom developed two staff infections and e-coli."

Aaron stopped talking for a moment as if collecting his thoughts. My eyes remained glued on him and I thought for a moment that he did not want to say more. However, after a few moments he continued.

"Mom's body became too weak to handle the infections so she ended up in critical condition. Her kidneys, bladder and liver started to shut down. The doctors decided to put her on the list for a new liver and it took about a month to find her one. It helped somewhat and gave her a bit of much-needed energy. She actually got to come home for a couple of weeks but she quickly grew weary. She also suffered a high fever so we rushed her to the emergency room and she was admitted into the hospital… again. Only this time, she never came home," he said dejectedly. "She just got sicker and sicker. Her organs began shutting down again and there was nothing they could do for her."

I felt my eyes grow bigger as I listened to his heartbreaking story. In response, I wrapped my arms across my chest and hugged myself. Then out of the blue, his face turned red and I could see the anger in his eyes. I jumped when his hand formed a fist and he punched the dashboard.

"Damn doctors!" he yelled. "They finally told us that the mesh they used had been recalled. It was already infected." He sucked in a deep breath and glared at the road ahead of us.

"My dad, as you can imagine, was devastated. He could not imagine living without her. The doctors asked him if she had a DNR order."

He turned to look at me and must have seen me wince, not understanding his words.

"A DNR means do not resuscitate," he explained. "In other words, they wanted to know if they should do CPR (cardiopulmonary resuscitation) and administer drugs to bring her back if her heart stopped."

"Ah, I see," I replied shaking my head.

"Well, my dad said yes, of course they should try to resuscitate her. He had been married to her for 30 years and was terrified that he might lose her." Aaron paused again and the pain on his face was evident. I saw him wipe a tear from his cheek before he continued.

"We were at the hospital visiting mom when she died." His voice trailed off and he closed his eyes for a moment. "The first time."

"What do you mean – the first time?" I asked, captured by his words and still staring at his grief stricken face.

"She died or so they said. I'm not a doctor but I watched them do CPR and give her a drug. When her pulse returned, I never saw my dad cry so hard. He stood next to her holding her hand and whispering her name but she never came round. That didn't stop him from talking to her and telling her how much he loved her.

Then the machine above her made these beeping sounds. The doctor and nurses had stepped out of the room when all of a sudden, the machine made a long, harsh sound and they came running back in. They pushed my dad out of the room and began CPR again but her pulse stopped a second time."

I could not hold back the tears that swelled in my eyes as I listened to him talk about this terrible tragedy in his life. It was difficult to imagine anyone going through something like that let alone having it happen to your own mom. I watched as his body slouched down and his hand whisked past his cheek wiping away more tears. Then he noticed I was crying too and apologized for upsetting me.

"No, Aaron. It's quite all right," I said reassuringly. "I'm just glad you felt at ease enough to share this with me."

To look at him, one would never know the burden he carried. I knew from the first time I met him that there was something special about him. He was such a caring and compassionate man. I found myself scooting across the front seat closer to him and placing my hand gently on his shoulder.

"I'm so sorry," I whispered. "No one should have to go through that."

Aaron tried to smile a little and shook his head but would not look at me.

"Anyway, after she died," he sniffled, "I tried to be around for my dad but he was so lost without her. Now, he doesn't even talk to me. Whenever I try to have a

conversation, he just sits in his chair staring at mom's sweater that hangs over her favorite chair."

Without thinking, I kissed him softly on the cheek like a mama bear soothing her cub. Aaron seemed to succumb to this and looked so helpless. We drove on in silence until we reached a forested area and he turned onto a dirt road. We had driven quite a distance but the time seemed to fly by. I still sat near him with my hand on his shoulder when he finally parked the car and shut off the engine. He turned toward me, and I saw that his eyes were bloodshot and streaks from his tears lined his face.

"I can't believe I just told you all of that," he said blinking. His looked deeply into my eyes, his face portraying a worried expression.

"I hope you don't think I'm foolish," he said. "I'm supposed to be strong. Men don't cry," he added leaning down to kiss my cheek, "but somehow you got into my soul and I bared everything. I've never done that before."

Aaron's words left me speechless. I stared into his eyes and smiled not knowing what to say. Finally, I turned to look in the back seat.

"You ready to get beat at fishing?" I asked to lighten the mood. Fortunately, the mournful moment vanished as he smiled widely - and those dimples peaked out at me again!

Chapter 8
A Day at the Fish Pond

"Come on," Aaron said as he hopped out of the car. "Show me what you've got, woman!"

I still resolved to show him that I was not as dainty as he thought. I could catch and clean a fish. Ugh! What was I doing? He handed me the army pants and boots to slip on while he did the same. Then he passed me the fishing rods, while he grabbed the tackle box and a small cooler. He imparted a wink before heading toward the woods. I walked behind him as we made our way through the forest and then we walked together through tall grasses and around trees. There was no path so I wondered if he knew where he was going. Sure enough, the grin on his face indicated that we had almost reached our destination.

We sauntered toward a small stream running over lots of little rocks and followed the stream upward until we came across some larger rocks where the water flew more swiftly over them like a miniature waterfall. Butterflies and birds flew aimlessly around in the trees.

"We're going down there," he pointed as he walked onward.

The sound of the rushing water was calming and peaceful. I watched as some tadpoles swam by in the water that rushed through the rocks. We waded in until we finally reached the spot he sought. I could tell by his look of recognition that he had been there before.

A rustic, weathered picnic table sat next to a worn pail with a hole in it. To the right, I noticed an old tree stump that looked as if it had been filed smooth and a circle of rocks with an old cooking grid sitting in the middle of it. The wind rushed through the leaves creating an enigmatic and mysterious effect while the sun played hide and seek through the trees.

Aaron placed the tackle box on the picnic table and asked me for the rods. He pulled a little jar with what appeared to be moving earth out of the tackle box and opened it. As he picked up a worm and one of the fishing hooks, I thought at first that he forgot he planned to make me do it. Then to my surprise, he plucked out another and dangled it in front of me.

"Ready to put the worm on your hook, Miss Fisher lady," he teased.

I closed my eyes, scrunched my nose and drew a deep breath before holding out my hand. Yes, I had told Aaron a bit of a fib. I really had not gone fishing since Grade 8 - after the incident with the snake. I actually was afraid of worms mostly because I did not want to hurt the little things by stabbing them with a hook but I could not tell Aaron that! Secretly, I hoped he brought some liver. Fortunately, he noticed my squeamishness and came to my rescue.

"I'll put this on for you, my lady," he said in a fake English voice and laughed as if he'd heard my thoughts.

I smiled and bowed my head as if in shame while he put on the worm and threw the line out for me - just like dad used to do. The water's strong current was something I had not dealt with before. Dad and I fished in ponds that lay still as glass, not running like a faucet. When Aaron threw out his line, we had to make sure they would not get tangled because of the current. It seemed awkward at first trying to keep the lines from crossing each other.

Before I knew it, I felt a tug on my line. I was immediately thrown into a tizzy like I used to with my father. As I screamed with delight, Aaron set down his rod and rushed over to help me. The current made our task a little more difficult but he held onto the rod as I turned the handle to bring in the line. Sure enough, a fish wiggled on the other end. Being a gentleman, he did not wait for me to take the fish off the hook. For some reason, I felt saddened when he threw it into the bucket.

"It's going to die," I whimpered.

"This is only a bluegill and this is what God made them for… fishing!" he exclaimed.

Quickly, he put another worm on my line before tossing it into the water again. The sun reflected off the water and twinkled like crystal as it moved with the current and the sound of the rustling water seemed somehow romantic.

"So tell me some more about yourself?" I asked while we watched our lines to keep them apart.

"What do you want to know?" Aaron asked tugging his line to the right.

"Tell me what life was like when you were growing up."

"Well," he began, his face brightening. "I loved living on the reservation. I grew up riding horses and I'm

pretty good at that, you know." He quickly glanced at me. "Can you ride a horse?"

"I rode a horse when I was on vacations with my parents," I replied with a shrug, "but I can't say I was any good at it."

"We didn't own any horses," Aaron continued, "but some of our neighbors had them and as the neighborhood boys and I grew up, we learned to ride. I had a lot of pets growing up too. We had cats that always had kittens and dogs that had puppies. There were so many, in fact, that our porch was full of bowls of water for the animals. I even had a pet deer for a while."

Aaron pulled his rod straight up and I saw a fish dangle in the air. He removed it from the hook and threw it into the pail. He seemed so comfortable in that environment as he bated his hook again and threw it back in.

"What else?" I asked hoping he would tell me more.

"When I was a kid, my dad taught me how to use a rifle and when I got older, we went into the woods to hunt for deer."

"You used to shoot Bambi?" I asked in a weak voice. I squinted my eyes against the sun trying to focus on his face and he laughed aloud.

"It's not like the cartoon, silly."

The water moved our lines closer again and Aaron's started to cross over mine so he waded into the shallow part to move his rod out of the way. He pulled up hard, his foot slipped and the next thing I knew, Aaron was sitting less than graciously in the water. The line, which by then had no hook, hung almost ceremonially around

his head. I laughed so hard that I thought I would pee my pants! After all, he was the professional, right?

Then I felt a tug on my line and hollered for Aaron to help me. He quickly sprang to his feet and rushed over to pull in the line. I had caught another one. Yippee!

"It seems like I've been talking about myself all day," he noted as we both threw our lines back into the water. "

"I had a pet rabbit once," I announced. "I called her Mrs. Cadbury, you know, like the chocolate bar. I had her for a couple of years and did not realize that rabbits grew so big," I noted lifting my rod in one hand and holding up the other to indicate its size. "But she started to get sick."

My voice dropped and I could feel the pain of that time all over again.

"I cried to my mom, who took my rabbit to a veterinarian. She was given a shot and intravenous and seemed more like herself for a couple of days but then she fell ill again. I held her and she was breathing funny so I called mom. She wrapped her up in a blanket and cuddled her while I petted her face. Finally, Mrs. Cadbury stopped breathing. Mom found a box to place her in and we buried her in the back yard. Then I placed a flower plant over her grave. That's one thing I dislike about life… death."

"Yeah," agreed Aaron, "but it *is* a part of it and we have to accept it. We can't stop it."

We both fell silent for a few minutes as I pondered the inevitability of death. Then a fish jumped out of the

water in the distance and Aaron quickly pulled in his line.

"Another fish!" he exclaimed.

I shifted my eyes toward him before feeling a tug on my line as well.

"Eee!" I screamed. "I have another one too!"

Aaron was busy taking the fish off his hook as I tried to pull in my line. I yanked it back and the fish flew into the air toward my face. I jerked out of the way as it swung in mid air and then I raced over to Aaron.

"Do you want me to take the fish off for you?" he asked tauntingly.

"Please," I begged. "I don't want to hurt it." I shrugged my shoulders and Aaron just laughed. Soon we had our lines in the water again and listened in silence to the mesmerizing sound of the water.

"So what were you going to school for?" I asked getting comfortable on a rock.

"At that time, I thought about being a teacher."

"What did you want to teach?"

"Got another one," Aaron said as he pulled in his line. "I'm not sure yet."

As I watched him stroll back to the bucket, I felt another tug on my line. Again, I screamed like an over exuberant schoolgirl.

I enjoyed a wonderful afternoon fishing and talking with Aaron. The conversation was easy even if the occasional fish sometimes interrupted us. I listened intently as he talked and realized that I had never shared so much with any man before. No one ever seemed so in tuned and interested in me either. And I don't think I

ever laughed so much. What a pleasant surprise to find that we could have so much fun together. By the time the sun began to dip into the horizon, we had a full bucket of fish. Aaron strode toward me and took the rod from my hand.

"Come on, Annette."

"Hey!" I squinted at him mischievously. "I'm having fun here."

"Sorry but it's time to clean these babies."

Not expecting that, I sat stunned and unable to respond.

"Don't worry. It's painless," he assured. "Help me find some twigs."

We paced around the grounds of our little picnic site and gathered up small branches. Meanwhile, the wind picked up sending leaves dancing through the trees. Aaron grabbed a couple of large branches and some twigs to build a small fire in a circle of rocks on the other side of the pail. I watched with interest as he set one fish on the old stump. This

seemed so natural for him. First he used a knife to cut off its tail. Then he scaled it and cut a line down the middle to remove the intestines and other internal organs.

"See how easy this is?" he said reaching for another fish. "Your turn."

Since I was not yet sure how he cleaned the fish, I stood motionless but he reached for my arm and led me to the stump. He slapped the knife full of yucky fish guts into my hand and I winced at the slimy feel of it. I did not look up at him but I'm sure he could see the horror on my face!

"Here," he said. "Let me show you again." He stood behind me and wrapped his arms around me.

"Hold the fish like this," he instructed taking my left hand to hold the fish in place. He took my right hand, which held the knife and showed me how to scrape off the scales.

I could not help being aware of his warm body so close to mine. I felt his breath on my neck as he concentrated on the fish cleaning procedure. I told myself to pay attention to the knife, not him but it was darn near impossible to do!

When we finished scaling the fish, he withdrew his arms and stood close to me. His eyes stayed on the fish but his arm brushed against mine as he worked causing my heart to flutter.

"Now, this is how you gut a fish," he said taking the knife and slicing it open.

Taking a deep breath, I decided to be a man about it. After all, I did want to prove to him that I could do anything he could do. He had another knife and after another training session, I felt more confident and cleaned a fish without his help. I think I impressed him and before long, all the fish were ready to throw on the old grid over the fire.

"Hope you're hungry," he said as he opened the cooler and withdrew two plastic plates along with some silverware.

As I watched him, I thought of the movie Mary Poppins. You know the part where she pulled all kinds of stuff out of her purse.

"Do you also have some food in there?" I quipped.

He looked up at me, winked and took out two bottles of water.

"My lady," he said in that fake English accent again while bowing down in front of me. "You are about to taste the best fish dinner in town."

Aaron had some salt and pepper packets, and sprinkled them on the fish as he cooked them. I sat by the picnic table and watched him perform his magic. While some of the fish sizzled on the grill, he placed the rest in a plastic bag he kept in the cooler. The fish smelled so good, as the wind carried the scent across the picnic table. When they were ready, we sat across from each other to eat.

"You seem to know your way around a camp fire," I said. "This fish tastes great."

"Thank you!"

While we ate in silence, I noticed that the temperature had dropped. The wind kicked up again and some leaves flew in circles around us. A couple of branches in the fire crackled sending blazing hot sparks into the air.

"I've got a hunch you've done this before," I said to renew our conversation.

Aaron's face turned a little pink and I was curious as to why.

"So how many girls have you brought here?" I asked nonchalantly, not wanting to sound jealous. "Did you

show them how to catch and clean fish?" My eyes peered into his waiting for an answer.

"Including you?"

"Yes, including me!" I replied with a giggle.

That smug smile reappeared on his face and he drummed his fingers on the tabletop as if counting in his head.

"Just one."

"Really?" I replied, not sure I believed him.

"I used to come here with my dad and we fished all afternoon. Then we cleaned the fish and brought them home. Mom would cook them so we could enjoy our freshly caught dinner. She knew just what spices to sprinkle on them to make them taste good. Sometimes, she soaked them in lemon juice before frying them in the pan. She was the one who taught me to use salt and pepper when I grill them."

Beginning to feel chilly, I crossed my arms and wrapped them around me for warmth. Aaron seemed to sense my discomfort.

"Ready for dessert?" he asked. "When you roast your marshmallows, the fire will warm you up."

He placed the cooler near the fire and we sat on the ground next to it. The strong breeze picked up the warmth from the fire and blew it across the grass… and thankfully, me. I shuffled my hands together gathering the heat. Aaron grabbed a couple of branches and scrapped off the leaves so we could use them to roast our marshmallows. As I held my stick over the fire, I listened to the crackling fire and watched the flames dance wildly. I preferred my marshmallow almost black so I let the

flame lick up and around it. Then I drew it to my lips and blew out the flames. Aaron had a small box of Graham crackers and a chocolate bar so we made Smores.

"I just love Smores!" I said gleefully.

We laughed as we tried to wipe the marshmallow off each other's mouths and before we knew it, the sun sat near the horizon.

"Are you ready to go back to the car?" Aaron asked wistfully.

I nodded and then frowned hating the idea of ending our date.

"Did you enjoy your dinner?" he asked throwing water on the fire.

"It was terrific," I replied as I helped to clean up our mess.

We wanted to leave the forest just the way we found it. Once done, we picked up our gear and headed to the car. Above us some clouds seemed to move a little faster, likely due to the wind. My long, thick hair blew around my face acting like a scarf and keeping me warm. Aaron grew quiet as I followed him so I concentrated on the sights and sounds

of the forest. I wanted to imprint everything in my brain so I could remember every moment of our day together.

"It's so beautiful here," I said when we reached the car. "I love the way the water runs amid the rocks and how the sun plays around the trees… peaceful, you know?"

Aaron knew the place well and likely took it for granted but for me, it was an amazing experience. Our adventure brought back fond memories of the trips I took with my mom to Mount Scott… always so peaceful and serene.

"Yeah," Aaron replied as he took the rods from me and set them back in the car. Opening the trunk, he placed our dirty army pants and boots inside. As we settled in the car, he turned to me with a dreamy smile. I nervously tucked a strand of hair behind my ear.

"Welcome to my world," he said taking my hand in his. "Thanks for coming with me."

Aaron's hand felt so warm and comfortable that I did not push it away. I liked the feeling and did not want to let go.

"Thanks for asking me."

As we drove off, our hands remained together and I recalled the terrific day we just shared.

"I can't believe that I only met you yesterday," I said. "I feel like I've known you much longer."

"I was thinking the same thing," Aaron replied turning quickly to smile at me.

I yawned and closed my eyes for only a second… or so I thought. Without knowing it, I fell into a deep sleep. When we reached my house, I woke up with my head on his shoulder. I think it was the stopping of the car that stirred me back to reality. I did not remember the drive and when I awoke, I recognized the neighborhood. I could feel my face turn warm and then red with embarrassment.

"Oh, I'm sorry," I whispered. "I really had a great time but I think all that fresh air wore me out."

"That's good to hear," he replied in a teasing tone. "I thought maybe I was a boring date."

For what seemed like an awkward moment, we sat still holding hands. Then I lifted my hand away and gazed into his eyes. What is it about him? I wondered. Why do I feel so drawn to him?

Aaron moved a little closer, his dark eyes hypnotizing me.

"I don't think I'll forget about this day for a long time," I murmured nervously. Then I quickly kissed him on the cheek and slipped out of the car. I watched intently as he drove away, my mind racing.

"Could I really be falling for a man I only met a day ago?" I whispered.

Chapter 9
'Me' Time

Monday mornings were 'me' time. The beauty salon was usually closed on Sundays and Mondays but on Sunday, my housemates were usually home making it difficult to sleep in. On Mondays however, they left early for classes and since I had taken the semester off, I could get some extra rest. Although they clamored about before they left, my box fan usually drowned out their voices and the thunder of footsteps on the stairs as they raced to get to school on time.

My pillow and blanket were so inviting as I cuddled in them and dreamed of the great time I had with Aaron the day before. At some point, I must have fallen back to sleep. An hour later, I awoke for a second time and all was quiet. Slipping out of bed and putting on my robe, I strolled into the living room where a couple of empty pizza boxes and a few cans of beer sat on the coffee table.

I live with a bunch of sloppy kids, I thought picking everything up and throwing it into the trash.

I poured myself a cup of coffee from the little they left me in the pot before they left. Moving to the kitchen table, I grabbed a chair, sat down and enjoyed the warmth of the cup between my hands. On Mondays, I followed a regular routine: clean the kitchen and my bathroom, and then do my laundry. This day, I sat up startled when the phone rang. I always talked with mom on Mondays, so I figured it must be her. She preferred to call that day because she said the noise was unbearable

on my end if she called at other times. Either that or the phone was busy when my housemates were home.

"Hello?" I said with a smile, always happy to talk with her.

"Good morning, sunshine. How is my favorite daughter doing today?" She always knew how to make my day brighter. I hugged the phone and sat back down again.

"Hey mom, how are you today?" I said hoping she sensed the sincerity in my voice.

"Good sweetheart. Not to put any pressure on you but I just wanted you to know that I miss you."

I heard her giggle in the background.

"I miss you to, mom. How's dad?"

"He's doing well and told me to send you his love."

"So how was your Sunday?" I sighed. "Did you guys do anything exciting?"

"I made your dad go with me to Mount Scott. I haven't been to the mountains since you left. Of course, he didn't climb the rocks with me like you always did but we walked around, enjoyed the view, and watched the young mothers and their children as they climbed. Then I made him take me to Meers," she added. "We had a very nice afternoon. What about you?"

"I had a date," I blurted out. I said it fast and with so much excitement that I actually covered my mouth after releasing the words.

"Really? Who is he? How did you meet? Where did you go? What time did you get back last night? Did you have fun?"

"Oh mom, I had so much fun and it's funny that you mentioned climbing the rocks. Aaron took me to a reservation and we did that. We also fished."

"Since when do you like to fish?" she asked laughing. "You haven't done that since you were in the eighth grade and went with your father."

"I know. I didn't think I would enjoy myself either but I gave it a shot and had such a good time. My date actually had us catch, clean and cook the fish."

Mom laughed so hard on the other end of the phone that I thought she might have a heart attack. When she calmed down she asked, "How did you meet him?"

"At the beauty salon, mom. He was a customer. I gave him a haircut and for my tip, he asked me out for lunch."

"Sweetie, is that very smart - to go to lunch with a total stranger?"

I could sense the concern in her voice and I wiggled uncomfortably in my chair.

"Mom, we just walked a few doors down the street from the salon. How much trouble could I get into?"

"Well, all right then. Tell me about him."

"He's really nice and seems quite gentle… and he sure knows his way around a camp fire."

Our conversation continued for the next half hour. I told her that Aaron was Native Indian and described his appearance. I also related what he told me about his mother's death. I tried to give her a picture in words of how beautiful the place was where we fished. As well, I noted that he went to church with me, and told her how Lynn and Jessica tried to talk me out of asking him.

"Well you know honey, it's important to have a man in your life that believes in God like you do."

I failed to mention that he usually did not attend church and that I thought he might be Catholic. At least that is what I thought when I saw him perform the sign of the cross and kiss his necklace after we prayed. Our mother/daughter talk ended with the same pleasantries as usual: "I love you. I miss you. Please stay safe. Talk to you next week."

After I hung up, I showered and cleaned my room. I decided to tackle the kitchen due to my sense of responsibility within the house. It was not like my four housemates expected me to clean up after them but I thought that since I was not in school, I could do a little bit more to help out. Heck, I had nothing better to do and I prided myself on not being lazy. I put in a load of laundry before I started cleaning the dishes. The house did have a dishwasher, so I rinsed the dirty plates before I placed them inside.

As I worked, my mind returned to the day before. I was angry with myself for falling asleep on the way home and wondered if Aaron would ever call me again. Of course, I hoped he would. I wonder if he's thinking of me too. I thought.

I needed to keep busy to stop everything from racing around inside my head. I swept and washed the kitchen floor, and folded my laundry. Then I ironed the clothes with wrinkles, hung them up and then decided to surprise my roommates by cooking dinner. Before I could do that though, I had to go into town to buy some chicken, lettuce and tomatoes.

I arrived back home around 2:45 p.m. and started to cook. I sprayed some oil into a frying pan and turned the stove on low. Then I found the cutting board and sliced up the chicken. At around 3 o'clock, I heard the front door open and Lynn strolled into the kitchen.

"Hi Lynn," I said over my shoulder while browning the chicken.

"Hey Annette. How's it going?" she asked walking toward me. She peered over my shoulder and into the frying pan. "Looks yummy. Are you going to share that?"

"Yes, silly," I giggled. "I thought I'd make us dinner tonight so how about a chicken salad?"

"Sounds great!"

Watching my parents cook and learning from them sure came in handy.

"So how was your day?"

"Good but nothing special," Lynn replied, "but I want to hear about your date yesterday?"

She made her way to the table and grabbed a chair. I detected in her voice that she was either a little jealous or perhaps, concerned. Grabbing a spatula, I turned the chicken before I shook on some garlic salt.

"I had a great time," I said finally. "What did you think of him?

"He's very cute, long hair and all," she responded in a cocky tone.

"He's Indian and lives on the reservation" I noted ignoring her somewhat uppity attitude.

"So how did you meet?"

Lynn's eyes focused on me like mother superior at a convent. I finished stirring the chicken and put the spatula down. My hands slapped my hips as I turned to look at her.

"You sound just like my mother."

"Well, I do feel a little responsible for you after dragging you away from that lonely army town," she said laughing. "Besides, I don't trust him… you know how naïve you are about guys."

I rolled my eyes as the front door slammed. I could hear footsteps and voices coming down the hallway. Jim was in the lead with Zack and Jessica following slowly after him. They were deep in conversation and Jessica sounded concerned. She noted that she had to pass all her classes with 90 percent and math was her toughest.

"Smells good," said Jim as he entered the kitchen.

"So you would really help me with my math and tutor me?" Jessica asked.

"Why not?" Zack responded. "After all, I am an expert on that subject."

Jessica leaned in and gave him a big hug. I glanced over to see the smile on his face until she pushed him away. He seemed to hug a little longer than she planned.

"I just need help with my math," she bluntly informed him. "Don't get the wrong idea."

"What did I do?" asked Zack grinning and attempting to look innocent.

"Hey guys, Annette's making us chicken salad for dinner," Lynn said smacking her lips to get their

attention. "And this girl sure knows how to cook. She learned from the best… her parents."

"Thanks," I replied blushing. I felt someone behind me and saw a hand reach out toward the frying pan.

"Yuck, rabbit food," Jim commented as he tried to sneak a piece of chicken.

My reflexes were fast. I slapped his hand and sent him sulking toward the kitchen table.

"No one is forcing you to eat what I cook," I responded harshly.

"Leave her alone," yelled Lynn. "I'm trying to get the scoop on Annette's date yesterday and all about her new lover boy."

"Did he kiss you?" teased Zack walking by and slapping me on the butt. I jumped not expecting that. I never saw him act that way before.

"Hey," I grunted. "I did not give you permission to touch me."

"Come on, girlfriend. You have a cute toosh."

"What?" I asked and the others echoed the word.

Zack slinked down on a chair as all three of us girls scowled at him.

"Fine," he said raising his palms forward. "I'll keep my hands to myself. I was only playing."

The girls and I glanced at each other and reading each other's mind, we all peered angrily at Zack again. He just shrugged his shoulders as if to say he already apologized. However, I was quite sure he would not try a trick like that again!

"Well, what happened yesterday," Jessica asked. "Where did you go? And by the way, he's really cute!"

I stood by the stove finishing the chicken as my four housemates sat around the table waiting for my response. Lynn sat up tall with curiosity in her eyes. Jessica placed one elbow on the table and held her head up actually looking a little bored. The boys sat casually with their backs slouched against the chairs. Perhaps they wondered if I kissed and told or maybe they were just hungry and killing time before dinner. Either way, I began by relating how Aaron and I met, how we ate lunch at the cute little deli and then reminded them that they met him before our date.

When the chicken was finally ready, I scrapped the meat out of the pan and into a bowl. That was a quiet signal for help so Zack got up and took plates out of the cupboard.

Following his example, Jim grabbed the silverware and glasses. Jessica scooted her chair out, went to the refrigerator for lettuce and fetched a knife to cut it. Lynn helped her and before I knew it, the salad was ready. I watched in awe as everyone pitched in to help and it made me a little homesick.

"Tomatoes anyone?" I asked pulling them from the fridge.

"Yeah, sure. That would be great," answered Lynn as I cut them up into tiny squares.

"Do we have any diet salad dressings?" Jessica asked. She was always watching her weight – not that she needed to do that.

"I didn't even look," I admitted.

Lynn checked the fridge, found a bottle and brought it to the table. As we settled in to enjoy our meal, Lynn coaxed me to go on with my story. I waited until we all had our salads together. It was a little noisy with please and thank you going back and forth, and food being passed around. Even Jim fixed himself a salad except that he put more chicken than lettuce on his plate. Finally, the only sound I heard was the scrapping of silverware on the plates.

I then spoke of our long ride to the reservation and how much we talked. I also noted that I was not aware of any forests nearby until he brought me to his favorite fishing spot. Lynn and Jessica seemed totally rapt as I described the beauty of the stream and the boys seemed to enjoy hearing about how we cut and cleaned the fish. Although Zack liked to fish, he said he never cleaned one before. After I explained how I used a knife, Jim stopped eating for moment and asked me to stand for inspection in case any part of me might be missing. That made everyone laugh. Finally, I related how I fell asleep on the way home.

I felt that I should keep some things about the date to myself. For instance, I did not share what Aaron told me about his mother and how she died. I also did not say that I might be falling for him or the fact that I wished he had called me.

That night when I went to bed, I tossed and turned, disappointed and angry with myself again for not staying awake to talk to Aaron. Yet I smiled as I relived the events of our date and was secretly thrilled to know that

he never brought any other girls to that fishing spot before.

Chapter 10
A Trip to Shawnee

I needed to be at work early on Tuesday because I had a customer arriving for a perm at 8 a.m. You see, at the beauty salon I could rent a chair and use my own supplies, in which case I would pay the owner monthly or I could work strictly on commission. I worked 60/40 meaning I paid the salon owner 40 percent of everything I made each week - except for the tips of course!

We did not punch a time clock but were assigned appointments. The idea was to get as many appointments as possible each day to make more money. We made more money when we did perms and hair colors than if we just gave a haircut or shampoo and set. Needless to say, I was happy that I had a perm scheduled first thing in the morning.

Since the woman's hair fell past her shoulders, I could charge her $100. She requested a spiral perm, so I would use special rods with a couple of boxes of perm solution. This job would definitely take me about three or four hours and I looked forward to it. I needed something to cheer me up since Aaron did not call. I really felt at that point that I must have messed things up with him and did not blame him for not calling. I would be mad too, if he had done that to me. In this case, I was only upset with myself.

I arrived at work about 7:45 a.m., a little early so I could set up for my appointment. My customer walked in right on time. The woman, whose name was Crystal was about 26 years old, tall with pretty brownish red hair. At

my station, I asked her about her hair. Crystal said she was tired of straight hair and wanted some curl. She added that when she set her hair in hot rollers, the curls always fell out in about an hour.

After we decided how tight she wanted the curls, I moved her to the shampoo bowl. Then while putting the spiral rods in her hair, I listened to the radio along with a couple of the girls talking to their customers about their escapades over the weekend. The phone rang every once in a while and Carol took new appointments. It took me about an hour to put in the rods because her hair was so long and thick but I was happy to keep busy so I would not think about Aaron. I actually missed him even though we'd just met.

As I worked, Crystal and I shared a pleasant conversation, which also helped. I learned that she was going to graduate that year with a bachelor's degree in nursing. When it was time to prepare the perm solution, I gave her a towel to place on her face. It would stop any drips from seeping into her eyes and hopefully, help a little with the sour egg smell of the solution. Carefully, I poured a small bottle of it on each rod, used up a second one and then placed a small plastic bag over her hair to let the solution cook. It would take about 20 minutes before I could check to see if her hair was curling properly. It was already 10 a.m.

"Annette, the phone is for you," yelled Carol.

I excused myself and sauntered to the front desk. I could not believe how nervous I felt hoping it would be Aaron. After Carol handed me the telephone, she left the desk so I could talk in private.

"Hello," I said quietly.

"Hey Annette, how are you?"

I thought my heart would leap out of my chest when I heard his voice. Leaning on the desk, I placed my elbow on it to hold up my head.

"Hi Aaron, I am doing fine thank you."

I tried very hard not to sound too elated but inside, my stomach stirred with butterflies. I even felt a little flushed and my hands got sweaty. Is this what it's like to be in love? I wondered.

"How are you today?" I asked hoping he could not sense my nervousness.

"I don't have much planned today and wondered if you wanted to go out again?"

In my excitement, my elbow slipped on the counter and I tipped over a can of pens. They scattered all over the floor. Completely embarrassed, I stooped and tried to pick them up while still holding the phone. I quickly realized that all eyes were on me but I just shrugged my shoulders and did not look up.

"What?" I asked to make sure I heard him correctly.

"You aren't mad at me or anything are you?"

"Uh no, why would you ask that?" I'm sure I sounded out of breath as I tried to pick up the pens while still talking.

"You sound kind of strange," he noted. "Are you all right?"

"Yes, yes of course," I replied standing up and trying to regain my composure.

"Well, do you want to go out again? I promise I won't make you clean any more fish."

The memory of our last date echoed in my mind and I laughed.

"Sure, I would love that."

"What time can I pick you up?"

I checked the schedule book and realized that I had a haircut to do at noon as well as a shampoo and style at 1 p.m. As noted, we did not have a time clock but if we wanted to make money, we needed to hang around the salon, even if we had no appointments. I never knew when someone might walk in and ask for a haircut or even a high dollar perm. After the appointment at 1 p.m., I had no more scheduled. I knew that I should be responsible and stay in case something came up but I really wanted to see Aaron.

Making a compromise, I grabbed a pen and put a line down after my name at 3 p.m. to indicate I would not take any more customers after that. The only thing that could mess up this plan was if someone walked in at 3 p.m. and it was my turn to take the person - but I would deal with that, if and when it happened.

"Is three too late?" I asked eagerly.

"Sounds good. See you then."

I waited until he hung up before I put down the receiver. My body stirred with both happiness and some anxiousness. I strode quickly to the timer to check how long it would take before I could wash the solution off Crystal's hair. The day seemed to drag on and I wished it would end more quickly. I finished my perm at 11:30 a.m. and Crystal got just the curl she wanted. She seemed quite pleased and gave me a ten-dollar tip.

The customer who wanted a haircut came in at noon as scheduled and I finished her hair in time for my shampoo and set at 1 p.m. It was actually a quiet day at the salon with only a few walk-ins. This made my heart jump for joy because it meant I could probably leave at 3 p.m. like I wanted. I engaged in conversation with all my customers and I tried to pay attention but was not really listening. All I could think about was Aaron.

I finished at 2:30 p.m., so I spent the rest of the time cleaning my station. I swept the floor, folded my shampoo cape and looked around to see what else I could do. I had so much nervous energy to get rid of and tried to calm down. To that end, I grabbed a book and tried to get lost in the story. Yet every five minutes, I found myself looking at the clock and wishing the time away.

Three o'clock on the dot Aaron walked in. He nodded at the manager at the front desk and walked straight to my chair. Betty and Veronica glanced up quickly and then looked at each other smiling.

"Hi," he said looking so handsome in front of me.

He wore a pair of jeans with a light blue polo shirt. His hair hung free on his shoulders and he looked so good that I could have melted right there on the spot. I stood up from my chair and put an arm around his waist.

"Hi," I smiled giving him a quick kiss on the cheek.

Aaron leaned back evaluating my expression.

"You look like you missed me," he said in a teasing voice.

"Perhaps I did," I blushed.

"Maybe I missed you too," he added touching my shoulder and sending chills down my back. "You ready to go?"

"Of course."

Actually, I would have gone anywhere with this man – but why? Was it simply the remarkable physical attraction or had Cupid finally found me?

As Aaron and I walked out to his car, he reached for my hand. His touch made me feel all was right with the world. I squeezed his hand to let him know how excited I felt. I hung on to his last words about missing me and could not have been happier as they echoed in my mind. We reached the car and he opened the door for me.

"I thought of going for a bite to eat? Are you hungry yet?" he asked before shutting my door.

I waited until he got in before I answered.

"I had a snack in between my customers so I'm not very hungry yet."

Aaron's eyes shot up to my face full of curiosity.

"Well, is there any place you'd like to go before we eat?"

"How about visiting your father," I suggested.

"Really?" he asked, his body visibly tensing.

"Yeah, really. Just for a little while before we eat."

He seemed to hesitate so I put a hand gently on his shoulder. Instead of looking at me, he turned and glanced out the front window.

"Please?" I begged giving him my puppy dog eyes.

He sighed aloud before putting the key in the ignition. He did not seem too happy but surrendered to my idea.

We both seemed in a good mood and since we had to drive to Shawnee, I talked about my morning and the customers I had that day. He listened attentively and nodded occasionally but seemed extra quiet and distant.

We pulled into his father's driveway next to a cute, little colonial style home. To the left side was a large garden with old corn stalks standing straight up and weeds overtaking an unkempt garden. On the front porch sat two rocking chairs and a swing. Aaron turned off the engine and fiddled with his keys before getting out.

"Remember I told you that my dad has not been himself since my mom died," he said in a hushed voice.

"Yeah," I replied staring at him. "But that doesn't matter. I want to meet him anyway."

"Why?" he asked sounding like a perturbed child.

"Because your mom died and now he's the only parent you have left. I bet he would like to know what you've been up to… and meet your new friend." I placed my hand gently on his cheek. "Please?"

Aaron shrugged with resignation. Through the screen door, we could see his father sitting in his favorite chair staring at an empty one across from him.

"That was mom's chair," Aaron explained.

We stood in silence for a few moments before he mustered enough nerve to open the door. He introduced me to Tom and he shook my hand nervously. He remained seated in his chair and I noticed that he had long, white hair tied back in a rubber band just like his son's. Tom's face seemed worn and tired with deep lines

carved around his eyes and mouth. After a moment or two of silence, I spoke.

"I'm sorry we didn't call first. Please don't be mad at Aaron," I said. "It was entirely my idea to come and see you."

"It's okay," he responded scanning the house. "Sorry about the mess."

"Did we catch you at a bad time?" I asked now shifting from one foot to the other.

"No," he replied glancing up at me and then at Aaron before his eyes went back to his wife's chair. "It's a pleasure to meet you."

For a moment, Aaron and I stood in awkward silence not sure what to say so I smiled at Tom hoping to put him at ease. Then I took Aaron's hand and offered a little squeeze to let him know everything was all right.

"Would you like something to drink?" Tom asked as if he suddenly thought he should play the part of a good host.

"No thanks, Tom. I'm fine," I responded scanning the room.

A buffalo skin rug lay on the floor in the middle of the room and a picture of an Indian with a couple of feathers on his head but dressed in a suit hung on one wall. On the television stood a family picture and on the coffee table sat a photo album. I let go of Aaron's hand and walked over to the TV to pick up the picture. Aaron's mother did not look Indian because her skin was white. My eyes strayed to the photo album and could feel his dad watching me.

"Do you mind?" I asked taking a seat on the couch and picking up the album.

"No, not at all," he replied.

Aaron's dad moved to sit down next to me and I opened it. Aaron reluctantly followed and sat on the other side of me. His dad's eyes gleamed as he surveyed the photos, and spoke of his wife and son. We sat for an hour looking at the pictures while his dad reminisced and explained what each one was about. Aaron's face seemed puzzled as if he could not believe I got his dad interested in something.

I learned that Tom met his wife in Oklahoma City and when he married her, she graciously moved to the reservation with him. She was only 21 when they married and the women of the tribe took her in like one of their own. They taught her how to embroider, plant a garden and can food. Soon what she learned became her hobby. She enjoyed creating a large garden and canning so much food that during the winter, they always had enough to eat.

Tom and his wife only had one son even though she tried to have more. She lost her second one at two months pregnant and a third at three months. Although they tried, she could not get pregnant again. The sadness in his face as he spoke of her was unmistakable. It was easy to see that he still loved and missed her terribly.

Aaron's eyes lit up and he listened with great interest when his father related their lives in the past, which included the years he grew up and the fun they all had. I learned Aaron was an inquisitive child, always getting into something. Tom spoke with passion when he talked

about their hunting and fishing adventures together, and it seemed that he truly missed those days.

Aaron's face registered surprised when his dad spoke of how proud he was of his son. I noted that he had his mother's eyes but the cheeks and face shape of his father. The last picture showed the three of them at his high school graduation. They looked so happy. I commented on how wonderful they looked before I closed the album and placed it back on the table.

When Aaron and I finally got up to say goodbye, I caught a smile from his dad that seemed to denote gratitude.

"Thank you for sharing your stories with me," I said leaning in to give him a hug.

He hugged me back and Aaron looked astonished.

"Come back again," Tom said with sincerity as we headed out the door.

Aaron and I walked side-by-side as we strolled back to the car. On the way to back to Norman, he seemed lost in his own thoughts.

"Thanks for taking me to see you dad," I said and caught a glimpse of a smile on his face. "He seems so nice."

"I'm glad you liked him."

"I did. He seems like a very gentle soul."

"That really means a lot to me," Aaron replied giving my hand a tender squeeze. "I mean how nice you were to him and how you got him to finally open up," he added, his voice cracking.

He squeezed my hand more firmly and then let it go. For a while, we sat quietly listening to music from the car

radio. My mind kept going over some of the things his dad shared and how much he loved his wife. The stories he shared about Aaron growing up and the pictures of him made me smile.

I also recalled what Aaron told me about his mother's death. I could not imagine what it would be like to lose my own mother. Then it occurred to me that I might have been intruding? After all, Aaron did not ask me to visit his dad; it was my idea. Nervously, I drew my hair up into a sloppy ponytail and then let it fall back down again.

Chapter 11
Laughter & Fun

"Well, are you hungry yet?" Aaron asked interrupting my thoughts. He quickly looked my way before his eyes returned to the road.

"I thought you'd never ask?" I grinned.

"What are you in the mood for?"

"How about a big, juicy hamburger?"

"Yum!"

I was somewhat taken aback when Aaron stopped at a grocery store and picked up a loaf of bread. I was under the impression we were going out for burgers but he told me that he had a surprise for me and to be patient.

We drove to a Burger King where we ordered a couple of Whoppers, fries and drinks to go. I already knew he was the spontaneous type from our fishing date but I had no idea what he had up his sleeve this time. We drove a little further while I tried to pump him for information but he just ignored me.

"Wait and see" or "you'll find out soon enough," he teased.

We drove into a park and from a distance I caught sight of a small lake, picnic tables and a playground. Aaron took a blanket out of his trunk and when we reached the water's edge, he laid it down for us to sit on.

"I thought you might like a picnic today," he said pleasantly.

"I have to admit, you bring me to some of the most interesting places," I responded glancing out over the calm water.

Ducks were swimming peacefully and a few birds flew overhead. Aaron handed me my burger and I took a small bite. My mind seemed more concerned about our relationship and the differences between us. Aaron grew up in the country and could take care of himself in the wilderness. I bet he would be able to sleep under the stars and never go hungry or thirsty… or become frightened. I grew up in a small, prim and proper town. Yes, I enjoyed running through the rocks at Mount Scott but afterward I could easily stop for a hamburger at Meers and sleep in my own warm and comfy bed. I did not think I could take care of myself in the wilderness and knew I'd be frightened by the slightest unfamiliar sound.

Aaron still seemed quiet and lost in deep thought. I hooked my arm around his before getting his attention.

"A penny for your thoughts?"

He glanced at me, smiled and gave me a playful nudge.

"I was wondering why you are here," he confessed.

"Because I grew tired of the small town I guess. I wanted more. I was not sure what I should do with my life, so I decided to attend college here and hopefully find out."

I noticed the expression on his face, which seemed to imply, that was not what he meant.

"I'm sorry," I sighed. "I'm here because I want to be here."

Aaron turned toward the water's edge. Letting go of his arm, I took another bite of my burger. I let my eyes follow his and spotted some geese swimming with the ducks.

"It's gorgeous out here."

"You haven't seen anything yet," he said with a mischievous gleam in his eye. He had finished his burger but left a few fries in his box. I popped the last of my fries into my mouth and placed an uneaten part of my burger back in the box. Then I stretched my legs out and turned to him.

"You want to know what I was thinking," I asked. His turned to focus on me.

"I was thinking how happy I am that you came into the beauty salon and Suzie didn't work there anymore. I'm glad I've been able to get to know you and enjoy your company the last couple of days. I knew I was missing something in my life. Now that I met you, I realize it was you."

He stared at me in amazement and I smiled.

"Spending time with you just feels... right. You're so easy to talk too just like it is supposed to be. Like with my parents or like yours - you know, just feeling comfortable together."

I slipped my hand into his allowing our fingers to intertwine. We sat peacefully at the water's edge watching the ducks that seemed to be swimming our way. The sky reflected a pretty blue with a few white clouds drifting by. We sat close to each other while the chirping of the birds grew louder, and I marveled at how everything seemed so new and wonderful to me. I felt so at ease, as if we had been a couple for some time. Spending time with Aaron made me wonder if he was the reason I moved to Oklahoma City. I knew I would never forget what had happened between us. As crazy as it

might sound, I felt he was becoming a vital part of my life.

Aaron grabbed the rest of his fries and threw them out toward the lake. Almost immediately, the ducks swam closer quacking loudly. When they reached the fries, they scrambled after them. Then he opened the bread bag and handed me a couple of slices. I stared at him confused and he formed a presumptuous smile.

"What's happening?" I asked as I caught sight of some ducks swimming rapidly toward the grass… and us!

"Quick" he shouted. "Break off some bread and throw them to the ducks or they'll stampede our blanket."

I could not help laughing as we both valiantly attempted to throw them into the air toward the water's edge. Aaron stood up and threw more bread, as some of them got closer to us. This drew the attention of other ducks in the water.

"Throw some more bread!" squealed Aaron.

For an instant, I envision what he might have been like as a child but quickly stood and followed his lead. Soon there were no more ducks on the lake. The ducks and geese squawked loudly as they fought with each other for small morsels and in the process, they left the water's edge covered with feathers. I must have counted at least fifty of them.

A few birds also decided to join the melee. They flew down and tried to capture some bread without getting caught by a goose. Some birds swooped down and caught

the bread in mid air. We could not throw the bread fast enough.

I don't remember ever laughing so hard. I tore off more little pieces trying to make this unusual spectacle last a little longer but like all good things it had to eventually end. We finally ran out of bread. At first a couple of the ducks wandered over to our blanket looking for crumbs but just as quickly, they ran off into the water. Soon the spot was duck free except for those feathers! I fell back on the blanket laughing, with Aaron following my lead. By the time we sat up again, we realized that dark clouds had gathered above us.

Remember I said Norman lay within tornado alley. All across Oklahoma, we worried whenever there were severe thunderstorms. In the horizon, lightening flashed. Quickly, Aaron grabbed our blanket and I ran with him to the car. In just moments, the ominous sky opened up releasing a soft rain. Aaron covered my head with the blanket until we reached the car and scrambled inside. As the storm grew stronger, leaves rustled on the trees and thunder echoed overhead.

"Do you mind sitting here until the rain stops?" Aaron asked.

"I've always loved thunderstorms," I responded as he pulled me close.

We watched the rain intensify into a steady downpour falling diagonally from the sky. The raindrops pounded the windows offering a hypnotic yet romantic sound.

"You're awfully quiet," I noted after several moments of silence.

"Sorry. Just thinking about tonight."

I had no idea what he meant.

"Good things, I hope."

"Yeah, good things," he replied but offered no explanation.

The storm seemed to reach its climax as another sheet of rain broke from the clouds. Lightning flashed again - closer this time - and the thunder crashed like a cannon ball. I winced and jumped in my seat. Then I scooted closer to Aaron letting my legs brush against him. He put his arm around me as if for protection and I wanted to stay that way forever. The closeness of his body caused goose bumps on my skin. I definitely needed to know if he felt the same way.

"Have you ever been in love?" I asked innocently.

"That question just came right out of the blue," Aaron replied.

With the storm swirling outside, he turned toward me and looked deeply into my eyes. I just shook my head, embarrassed to tell him what I was really thinking.

"I don't think so," he murmured.

"You're not sure?" I asked amused.

"I dated a girl a couple of years back and at the time, I thought I might be in love. Mm… that's what I told myself anyway… but now when she comes to mind," he added sweeping some hair from my shoulder, "I think I only cared for her and enjoyed spending time with her. When we weren't together, I didn't find myself missing or thinking about her."

I sat quietly taking in his answer and felt satisfied by it. We looked out the front window in silence listening to the rain.

"How about you?" he asked.

"No," I said instantly.

"Well, you must have known someone you liked - somebody you enjoyed being with." His expression revealed that he did not believe me. My eyes traced the curve of his face as he talked.

"I dated a few guys but no one I could not live without," I replied smiling.

"Are you sure you didn't date anyone you thought you might be in love with?"

I knew he was fishing and rightfully so. It was his turn to interrogate me. My mind traveled back to high school and my best friend Lynn, who seemed to know the boys better than I did.

"In high school, I found the boys immature and only seeking notches on their belts. I grew up believing you only gave yourself to your husband. Remember, I came from a small town. My mother only let me go out in my junior and senior years of high school."

I hesitated before I continued, gauging Aaron's reaction. His eyes remained glued on me waiting for more. I knew my explanation would sound lame but said it anyway.

"My girlfriend, Lynn, always warned me about the guys that asked me out and I was smart enough to listen and believe her." I sighed. "If she said not to go out with someone, I heeded her warning."

"Did she warn you against me?" Aaron asked with a puzzled look.

I peered out the front window without responding, trying to find the right words. I watched the rain still

pouring down, although it had slowed along with the wind. I swallowed to cool the sudden dryness in my throat. Then I looked at Aaron, the car roof, to my feet and back to him. I had to be honest.

"She told me she found you a little reserved and quiet. She said those were the kinds of guys you needed to watch out for."

I felt my hands become sweaty and part of me was not sure I should have told him so much.

"Anything else?" Aaron sighed.

"Yeah," I almost whimpered. "Zack doesn't trust you either." My eyes dropped to my hands as I tried to wipe the perspiration on my pants.

"Of course, he would agree with Lynn," Aaron laughed. "He wants to go out with you." Suddenly, his smile disappeared and he became more serious.

"I'm glad you didn't listen to Lynn this time… I promise to be a perfect gentleman."

"Huh?" I said turning toward him.

"Tonight. Tomorrow night. Whenever. I'm not like any of those guys."

I traced a finger along his jaw from his ear to his chin and felt my skin tingle.

"I know," I said amused. "Why do you think I'm with you now?"

It grew quiet for a moment and I felt that I must have embarrassed him.

"From the first time I saw you, I only felt honesty and tenderness come from you," I said.

Aaron turned away without responding. I could not figure out his expression. He seemed to be torn.

"I'm sorry if I made you uncomfortable," I whispered. "Sometimes I blurt out what I think without taking into account how it might come across to other people."

"You didn't make me feel uncomfortable," he replied placing a hand on my shoulder. "It's just that I've never had anyone say something like that to me before. You have no idea how much the last few days with you mean to me." He moved closer and whispered, "I love you."

My heart began beating so fast. I could not believe I heard those words from Aaron.

"I'm scared," I confessed and Aaron drew me close.

"You don't need to say you love me back."

"But that's why I'm scared, Aaron. I do love you."

His eyes looked longingly into mine and he caressed my cheek. As he drew me in, our lips met. I knew this was love - the kind that would last forever.

When the rain finally stopped and the sun went down, the air felt significantly cooler. However, the moon shone across the lake creating diamond shimmers and sometimes a star twinkled from behind a cloud. It was such a beautiful night. When Aaron finally brought me home, we stayed in the car a little longer as he held me and we kissed passionately.

That night when I went to bed, I could still feel my adrenalin pumping. I was obsessed with Aaron and enjoying every moment of it. The next morning, I arose with a smile on my face and hummed away happily as I got ready for work. I smiled at my roommates even before I poured myself a cup of coffee and I sang at work, even dancing around my station to the music on the radio while waiting for customers. The other employees

laughed aloud but seemed jealous because they could not share my happiness.

Over the following week, Aaron often called to check what time I finished work so we could go out for dinner and talk. One night, he took me to the movies to watch Forrest Gump. We sat in the back row where no one could see us and stole kisses now and then. Another night, I asked him to stay and visit with my roommates for the evening. We played Monopoly, ate pizza and had a wonderful time. By the weekend, Aaron's appearances at work and at my house became a common place.

On Saturday night, he planned to pick me up and attend church on Sunday morning. It was probably the greatest week I ever experienced. My feelings for Aaron grew by leaps and bounds. I never knew I could feel that way. When Monday morning arrived and my mother called like she usually did, I told her how happy I felt and related more about Aaron. I talked with so much energy and enthusiasm that I don't think I let mom say a word.

Chapter 12
Unexpected News

Around noon, I heard a knock on the front door. When I opened it, I saw Aaron standing with one hand behind his back. He looked so good in his jeans and button-down, gray shirt, which hung loosely around his slim body. His hair lay freely but was combed neatly down around his shoulders. His smile was enchanting as he stood waiting for me to ask him in.

"Are you hiding something?" I asked trying to peer over his shoulder.

He leaned in and gave me a soft kiss on the lips before he brought out the flowers he held. I quickly gave him a hug and told them how beautiful they looked. Then I ran to the kitchen, my heart pounding so fast at the sight of him.

Aaron followed me, half smiling and without the usual beat to his step. I immediately sensed that something was wrong but let it go. I showed him where the flower vase was on the top shelf of one of the cabinets and he reached up to get it. I cut the stems of the colorful carnations while he filled the vase with water. As I set it gently on the table, he asked me if I felt like getting away for a couple of hours.

"You hungry?"

"Sure," I replied. "What do you have in mind?"

We jumped into his car and drove to the deli - the first place we ever ate together. The woman behind the counter smiled with her usual graciousness when we entered.

"Hey Aaron. How is your dad doing?" she asked while readying our order.

She slapping the meat on the bread and talked without looking up. "We miss him."

"He's much better," Aaron replied.

I detected a hint of sadness in his voice. I had not heard that tone since he talked about his mother. I looked up at him confused. He shot me a half smile again, obviously hoping to convey that all was well. We sat and talked with ease but I sensed that something was off. When we finished our meal, he cleaned up the table and told the owner goodbye. Then he walked over to the counter and extended his hand for her to shake.

"Thanks for being such a good friend, Thelma," he said not letting her hand go.

"I have known your family a long time," she responded. "It was tragic what happened to your mother."

I thought I saw a tear form at the corner of her eye.

"I'm glad to hear your dad's doing well," she added withdrawing her hand and wiping her face. "Don't be a stranger… hear?"

"You will always have a special place in our hearts," Aaron noted as he walked toward the door. "Goodbye."

I followed him with the uneasy feeling that he was saying goodbye forever. Maybe it was his tone or the fact that he walked up to shake her hand. We got back into the car and Aaron said he did not want to take me back home yet. I spotted a loaf of bread on the back seat, which gave away our destination. Aaron seemed depressingly quiet as he drove, his mind preoccupied and

his eyes never straying from the road. When he reached over and took my hand, I felt so warm inside and thought that perhaps my fears were all in my head.

When we drove inside the park, he asked if I would like to walk around the lake. Some children ran around the nearby playground and slid down the slide with their mothers frantically asking them to be careful. A couple of kids sat near the water watching the turtles swim by. We walked to the water's edge and Aaron handed me some bread to feed the ducks as we strolled along. I could hear their quacking but did not pay much attention to them this time. If Aaron's weary expression was any indication, something was definitely wrong.

We finally found a picnic table and he climbed on top to sit.

"Are you okay?" I asked.

"No," he replied and my heart clenched into a tense ball.

If that sounds familiar, it's because this was the day my world went into a tailspin. Although Aaron claimed to love me, he announced that he was leaving to attend a boot camp at Fort Jackson in South Carolina. I had fallen for Aaron so hard in such a short time and this news literally ripped my heart out.

"It doesn't have to be over," I protested. "We can write and talk on the phone now and then… and when you come home on leave, I could see you."

I could not control my trembling body. A couple of flies flew past my face and I swatted them away. Not too far away, a mother called to her crying child.

"It won't be the same," Aaron said resignedly. "I won't be able to look at you every day, walk with you or feed the ducks with you. I won't be able to sit down and share secrets with you and I won't feel your arms around me like I do now."

I turned away feeling a rising sense of frustration and panic. Everything he said was true and my world, as I knew it, was about to change forever. I pictured the first time we visited the park with the ducks all around us scrambling for bread. I never laughed so much. Now, I felt like crying.

"I don't want to say goodbye," I said, the first tears gathering in my eyes.

In the distance, I could hear the ducks and geese so I knew someone was feeding them and a couple of kids began crying when their mothers tried to take them home. I felt like crying too but for an entirely different reason.

"I don't either," Aaron said as we both stared out at the lake.

It seemed like a long time that we sat in silence after that. Finally, the sun began to set and the air felt cooler.

"You ready to go?" he asked when I began to shiver.

He put his arm over my shoulder and nudged me to follow him. We walked to the car and he pulled his jacket out from the back seat placing it carefully over my shoulders.

"Thank you," I said, my voice squeaking.

My eyes started to blur with tears. I told myself I was not going to cry. After all, he did tell me the first time I met him that he spoke with a recruiter. At that time, my

stomach tied into knots but we never broached the subject again. He never shared what the recruiter said or what branch he would join so I did not ask or even think about the possibility that he might end up leaving me.

To be honest, a part of me was angry. Why didn't he tell me he decided in favor of the army? Yet part of me was terrified that I might never see him again.

"I didn't want to tell you…" was all he could say before I released my anger.

Immediately, my expression hardened.

"What?" I yelled my jaw tight. "You were going to leave and not let me know! You should not be surprised that I'm so upset, Aaron."

I pulled away from him with my eyes staring downward. Then I crossed my arms defiantly in front of my chest. To think I trusted this seemingly gentle and honest man. Perhaps Lynn was right and he was just like all the others.

"Why didn't you tell me you joined the army earlier?"

"We really haven't known each other that long," he said shrugging his shoulders.

All kinds of thoughts raced through my mind. Why did he pretend to be interested in me in the first place? How could he say he loved me? And how could I be so stupid to believe his every word? He attempted to pull me closer but I stood my ground and would not budge.

"I didn't want to tell you until the very last minute. I thought if I told you on Wednesday, we could enjoy the last couple of days together but I realized that you would

be working and hoped that if I told you sooner, you could take those days off so I could spend them with you."

He stopped, sighed and dropped his hands to his side.

"Annette, I had no idea that I would fall in love with you so fast. I was having such a great time getting to know you; I guess I put the army thing on the back burner so it wouldn't get in the way."

"I hate this," I said, my throat dry and beginning to hurt. I did not want Aaron to see my tears, so I turned away slightly.

"Me too," he confided moving closer to me. "I'm so sorry."

I tried to talk but no words came out. I leaned into his body and hid my face in his chest as my tears finally let loose and flooded down. He held me close and I could feel his breath on my neck. His arms were comforting but all that did was increase my anguish. I did not want him to go.

That night as I lay in bed, I felt a huge gaping void in my heart but Aaron had not even left yet. I tossed and turned for several hours as I tried to make sense of it all and eventually, I cried myself to sleep.

Chapter 13
Return to Mount Scott

Despite the fact that Aaron would soon leave for the army, we hoped to make the best of it and made plans to hike at Mount Scott. I wanted to show him the place where I shared so many days and memories with my mother. He said he wanted to know all about me so this seemed like the perfect place to take him. I called into work and told them I wanted the next couple of days off. I knew how irresponsible that sounded but I only had a few more days to spend with Aaron – to hear his voice and savor the feeling of his warm and loving arms around me. I also knew I would have to set aside my worries – and my tears - if I expected to enjoy this time with him.

I made a picnic lunch - nothing big - some sandwiches, apples, cookies and a couple of bottles of water. I did not plan to go into Lawton, only Mount Scott to hike and share the little time we still had together. Aaron arrived at 9 a.m. and when he kissed me hello, my heart skipped a beat. I ran to the kitchen to fetch the food-filled cooler and he followed me.

"My lady," he said bowing down in front of me. "Let me carry that for you."

We quickly scampered off to the car and our trip began. We had at least a two-hour drive ahead of us.

"Tell me more about what you'll be doing in the army?" I asked as he drove. "I had no idea what branch you decided to join or where you'll be going?"

A smile spread across his face manifesting those cute dimples I quickly came to adore.

"I enlisted in the army," he stated calmly, "because I want to defend our nation. I'm good with a rifle and I want my father to be proud of me. I want you to be proud of me too," he added quickly glancing my way. "I was told that I would be active for four years and inactive for another four. I want to see if I like the army enough to make a career out of it. Of course, they will own me for a while but I will get leave time and plan to spend it with you."

His hand found mine giving it a tight squeeze and I smiled in return.

"If I had known I would meet you and fall in love, I would never have signed up but this process began before we met."

I leaned over and kissed Aaron's cheek.

"I go to Fort Jackson first for basic combat training and will be away for ten weeks. I'm not use to someone telling me when to get up in the morning or when I can eat but I will have to get use to it," he said with more than a little sarcasm behind his words.

"That doesn't sound like fun at all," I noted wrapping my hand around his upper arm.

"It isn't supposed to be fun, silly. I will have to work hard taking part in a lot of physical exercise and schoolwork. But my recruiter said that since I have some college behind me, I could make sergeant faster than some of the others."

He flexed his arm and my fingers moved with his muscle as he showed me his strength and I laughed. The working out part should not be so difficult for him.

"One advantage I will have is that everyone in my platoon will be new like me. Some might be younger but we will all start fresh attempting to do the best we can and trying to outrank each other." Aaron paused and sucked in a deep breath.

"Next will be AIT, Advanced Individual Training," he explained. "This will involve expert training in a specific field where I'm placed, which can last anywhere from six to fifty-two weeks. Since I don't know where I'll be put yet, I have no idea how long I'll be gone or where I might be."

"Is that also going to be in South Carolina?" I asked peeking up at him from under my bangs.

Aaron smiled, threw back his head and shrugged his shoulders.

"Who knows?" he chuckled. "This is all new to me. I have no idea where they might send me."

As Aaron continued to talk about the army, he beamed with enthusiasm. I did not want to take that away from him, so I listened intently. He related more about his conversations with the recruiter and how his father responded when he finally told him his plans.

"How did your dad take the news of you leaving this week?"

"I'm really not sure. I first told him I was mulling over the idea was about six months ago. At that time all he said was, 'you do what you have to do,' so I figured he

was all right with my decision," he said drawing in another deep breath. "But I told him last night that I would be leaving this week and he seemed sad, as if he lost mom and now would be losing me. I assured him that I'd be back and he could write me in the meantime but I could not read his true thoughts."

I considered his words and images of his dad flashed in my mind. How upset he was when his wife died and how unsettling this news must have been. I let my head drop on his shoulder and stared straight ahead.

"Then he asked me about you," Aaron added much to my surprise.

"What?" I asked raising my head and facing him.

"He said you were a nice girl and wondered if you would wait for me. He said I should try not to lose you because you could keep me young and alive," he noted and then paused for a moment. "And you know, he's right."

Tears bubbled behind my eyes but I did not want him to see my cry. His words were the kindest I had ever heard. I laid my head on his shoulder again and wiped my eyes hoping he did not notice. I decided to move the subject on to lighter topics until we finally found Highway 49. When we arrived at Medicine Park, we drove up to the entrance of the refuge. Up ahead a herd of buffalo was crossing the road. What a sight it was as we waited for them to amble to the other side! We did not get too close fearing they might charge toward us if they felt threatened by our presence.

Driving through the refuge, we found the sign and started up the winding road to Mt Scott. We stopped at each pullout to take in the view. I was not sure if the countryside's beauty stood out more that day or if it was the company that made the sight so magnificent.

A sign at one of the pullouts informed visitors that Mount Scott was the second-highest mountain in the Wichita Mountains Wildlife Refuge at a height of 2,464 feet (751 meters) above sea level. The three-mile paved road around it gave the impression that the mountain was much larger than it was in reality. Turns on the road curved sharply and not all of them had fences to keep vehicles from falling to their doom. Aaron seemed exhilarated driving so close to the edge, which made me rather nervous.

We finally reached the top and decided to eat our sandwiches before going on our hike. With water bottles in hand, we set out on Long Horn Trail, which was two miles long.

Aaron pointed up to the sky wondering aloud whether the bird flying over us was hawk. His enthusiasm caused mine to increase as well. The wilderness around us was a sight to behold. The sound of the wind bustling through the trees and the amazing wildlife made it come alive. We observed a chipmunk as it scampered by and spotted a flock of birds flying from a nearby tree. The air seemed so cool and fresh - nourishing to the soul. Fortunately, I remembered to bring my jacket.

Aaron carried himself well without missing a step, even though I sometimes fumbled on a rock or large twig. His face lit up as he strolled easily down the path dodging

rocks. Along the way, he pointed out different trees and bushes as well as any creepy crawlers. We talked little, opting instead to enjoy the walk and Mother Nature. I hoped to remember and treasure these moments forever.

This journey was much different than going with my mother. We usually drove to the top of Mount Scott and climbed over some rocks to our favorite tree by the edge. From there, we could take in the beauty of God's creations. With Aaron, it seemed more of an adventure as we took in the sights and breathed in the wonderful mountain air. I pushed the thought that we only had one more day together back into my mind, not wanting to spoil our precious time together but sometimes I caught myself staring at him as he strode ahead of me, his hair flowing freely. I measured his body, imprinting it in my memory.

Whenever he noticed me lagging behind he yelled, "Come on, slow poke. We don't have all day. There's so much more I want to see."

I would instantly leave dreamland to catch up with his beckoning hand.

Our path became covered with large boulders that we had to climb and being a true gentleman, he helped me up and over them. The reward of our effort became clear when we witnessed the breathtaking beauty of the scene below. When we finally made it back to the car, we realized we were starving. Grabbing an apple I had packed, Aaron listened to my directions. There was so much more that I wanted to show him.

We headed east on Highway 49 until I asked him to stop. He slipped out of the car with me in tow and we

wandered over to a wooden fence. I took his hand and we spied a prairie dog standing on his hind legs eating something with its paws. Then another one popped its head up from a hole in the ground, while yet another scampered in the dirt. One of the dogs stopped and gawked at us seeming to evaluate us before rushing to another hole and disappearing inside.

Aaron laughed at the sight while squeezing my hand with delight. Then he leaned over, kissed me softly and thanked me for bringing him there. We returned to the car and drove on long winding roads through the mountains. Eventually, we arrived at the remains of the town of Meers. Much had changed since my younger days. Aaron came alive as he beheld the broken down, wooden buildings that had withstood time. He also noticed lights inside the buildings that were so time worn with paint chipping outside the once-colorful structures.

We walked up the worn wooden staircase to the porch, which surrounded Meers Restaurant. I was surprised to see that the elderly Indian gentleman was still there. He stood with one foot resting on a bench to display his snakeskin boots. Aaron insisted on stopping to talk with him. At times, he became animated as the old man shared stories about the various tribes. I could not help smiling.

Once inside the restaurant, we followed the hostess to our seats. We passed through a narrow hallway where the remains of an old desk and the post office could be seen. Instead of wallpaper, the corridor was covered with countless business cards that had been stapled over the years so they would not fall off. It was definitely not fancy inside. In fact, you could see the water pipes across

the ceiling but people did not come for the scenery inside the building; they came for the charm and the food.

We ordered our burgers and drinks. When they arrived, we received our drinks in the old glass canning jars. This amused Aaron because his mother used to can food all the time. The burgers were huge and greasy - just the way he liked them. As we ate, we talked about our day so far and everything we had seen. We also discussed where we should go next. We held hands across the table and quickly became lost in each other. Never once did we raise the reality that he would be gone in just one day.

We decided to drive to the Holy City where we walked into the church and Aaron put some change into a donation jar. He was quiet, I believe saying a prayer because I saw him perform the sign of the cross and kiss his necklace like he did before. Afterward, we wandered off to explore the grounds. I grew up in the area so nothing was new to me but I watched Aaron's ecstatic facial expressions as he took in the sites.

He spotted a rock building with a sign indicating that it was Mary & Martha's house, and another with a sign that read Bethlehem's Inn. Up ahead, a rock structure resembled the castle where the Roman governor, Pontius Pilot, brought Jesus Christ to trial before his crucifixion. Rocks had been placed together to display Jesus' manger and crosses stood where He was crucified. Aaron grew quiet as we walked with arms around each other's waists. Later he told me that his mother would have loved to see the Holy City.

When it was finally time to go home, I sat in the car and nestled close to Aaron. He took my hand firmly in his. Leaving the refuge, we just had to stop and gaze at a couple of Longhorn we saw at the side of the road. What a wonderful way to end an amazing day!

We drove in silence for a while, our individual thoughts taking over. A strange peace and acceptance overcame me about Aaron leaving but I still had questions. After some time, my curiosity got the best of me.

"Aaron," I asked, "what necklace are you wearing?"

He pulled a gold chain out from under his shirt. Attached to it was a picture of a woman and the words: "Oh Mary Conceived Without Sin. Pray For Us."

"I don't understand?"

"My mother was a devout Catholic and I actually attended a Catholic school for a few years when I was young," he explained. "We honor Mother Mary as Jesus honored her. We believe the blessed virgin can intercede for us, if we pray to her and have God our Father hear our needs."

I glanced up at him strangely. I had been told that I was a woman of many faces and could not hide what I felt, so I guess he read my confusion.

"I know," he said, "you're wondering how I could talk like that after telling you I gave up on church." Aaron drew in a breath and released it slowly.

"I went to church, and lit candles and knelt to pray for hours when my mom was sick. I pleaded for her life and even tried to make a deal with God but He let her die anyway. Because of the odd and unexpected reason for her death, I felt I had every right to be angry for a while – at least until I found the answer to this useless death. It isn't like she had cancer or got into a serious car accident and they couldn't revive her. It happened because the doctors messed up," he said, the pain written on his face again.

I could feel the love Aaron had for his mother as well as the agony he still felt inside. He became quiet and I hid the tears that sat just under the surface my eyes. I could not imagine how I would feel if something like that happened to my own mother. I pushed the thought out of my head because the tears threatened to gush outward. I did not want to talk about this anymore and let it go.

We drove quietly watching the sun disappear into the horizon. Aaron turned on the radio and the tunes took over the silence but our minds seemed to drift elsewhere. I lifted my head and kissed him gently on the cheek. He smiled and let my hand go so he could put his arm around me. He pulled me close while I rested my head on his shoulder watching the shining stars that soon peered out in the darkened sky.

I never wanted to leave this spot and wished he could hold me forever. At this point, we did not need to talk. I could sense his love just by his touch and wanted to remember this day always. I recalled the events earlier in the day and the fun we shared. It was amazing how the time just flew by. Finally and yes, too soon we arrived in front of my house. It was a truly sad moment because I did not want the ride or our time together to end.

"Thank you," Aaron said before kissing my forehead.

"For what?"

"For being you. If it weren't for you, I would not have been able to talk about my mother. If it weren't for you, my dad would still be silent and sulking. You opened up some doors, helping us to understand and talk about the pain and frustration we felt."

He kissed my neck and then my ear. I leaned back to get a glimpse of his face.

"Tomorrow?" I asked.

"Duh," he teased. "Early because I want to spend the morning with you and the evening with my dad."

He drew me close and our lips met. His tender kiss sent goose bumps down my body. I slipped out of his arms and the car with the promise to see him yet one more time.

Lying in bed that night, I recalled each moment of our day and tears fell on my pillow. I knew that somehow, I had to realize that even though Aaron would be away from me, life would still go on. Yes, it would be hard but we would see each other again.

Then I sense a kind of magic in my heart. I loved him and he said he loved me. I believed him with every breath I took. This relationship was not over and we could make it through this difficult time. I did not want his departure to be miserable, so I decided to write him a letter. After all, I would not have his address until he wrote, and that would not be until he found out what unit he would be in and where. I found some scented stationary and searched for a recent picture of myself. Then I sat on my bed, wiping away teardrops as I began to write.

Dear Aaron,

I want to tell you that I am so happy to have gotten to know you. The time I spent with you has been the happiest of my life. I did not believe in love at first sight but now I do. When I first met you, I felt something for you that I'd never experienced before and it has grown so much. I wish I were with you now. I miss the feel of your arms around me and your sweet kisses.

Going to Mount Scott with you was an entirely different adventure for me. Seeing it through your eyes revealed all the beauty I had been missing. I loved sharing your world and you sharing mine. It hurts to know that I could not be with you more before your new journey but know that you are in my prayers.

I want to thank you, Aaron, for sharing the devastating news about your mother and trusting me to share your heartache. My heart broke with this news but I know God is holding you in his arms during this tender moment. Please Aaron, I hope in time you will forgive God.

Wherever you are and whatever you're doing, please don't forget about me. It hurts me so that I won't be seeing you for a while but please know that you're in my heart and I hope I will always be in yours. I will be waiting for you.

I love you Aaron. Please be safe and come home to me. I can't wait to get your first letter.

Love, Annette

Wiping my face with the back of my hand, I placed the letter and my picture in the scented envelope. Sealing it closed, I put on some lipstick and kissed the back of it.

Then I nestled in my bed, closed my eyes and cried myself to sleep.

Chapter 14
A Tearful Goodbye

I awoke with a hollow emotional numbness inside and knew this day would be bittersweet. Even so I could not wait to hold Aaron in my arms one more time. As I dressed, I felt queasy. Glancing in the mirror, I noticed my swollen eyes and how bloodshot they looked from crying the night before. I could not let him see me that way so I dabbed a little Preparation H under my eyes - something I learned from the girls at the beauty salon - and some eye drops to help the redness subside before he arrived.

When the doorbell rang, Zack answered the door. I listened to the muffled sound of "Good to see you again," and "sorry to hear you're leaving for the army tomorrow." Then I heard Jim's voice and the thunder of shoes on the stairs as Lynn and Jessica ran down them. I imagined the handshakes from the guys and hugs from the girls as they politely said goodbye.

"Hey Annette," Lynn said knocking on my bedroom door. "You up? Aaron's here."

"Thanks, I'll be right out," I mumbled.

I needed to regain my composure. I took a deep breath as a few tears started to form. Blinking, I tried to get rid of them and wiped away the ones that managed to escape. I decided to wait until my roommates left because I did not want them to see me in such distressed.

"She'll be right out." I heard Lynn say. "Make yourself at home."

I waited until the front door shut for the last time. The house was then quiet so I opened my door. Aaron was sitting on the couch with his beautiful smile and adorable dimples ready to greet me.

"Why so glum?" he asked standing up.

I leaned into him and closed my eyes. He traced my jaw with his finger from my ear to my chin before leaning in for a kiss. A single tear trickled down my cheek.

"No more tears," he insisted gently wiping it away. "You hungry?"

"Yeah," I said trying to appear brave.

"Good. So am I. Come on, let's get some breakfast."

Aaron took me to a pancake house and sat next to me in a booth. We became lost in each other with conversation - so much that the waiter came to our table a couple of times before we even opened our menus.

After breakfast, we drove to the park and strolled around the lake, throwing bread out to the ducks. After all the bread was gone, we walked with our arms locked together. The sky was a lovely blue and the sun's warm rays peeked out from behind big, fluffy white clouds. We stopped to face each other, our arms wrapped tightly and bringing us close.

"What time do you fly out tomorrow?" I asked attempting to hide the sadness inside.

"Early," he replied. "I should be at the airport before you even wake up."

"And you're spending tonight with your dad, right?"

"I was planning on it. I also have to finish packing."

We had discussed that the other day but somewhere deep inside I hoped for a miracle –that he'd changed his mind about leaving me. I did not want to let him go but plastered a fake smile on my face as we walked around the lake. It seemed like only a matter of minutes before we finished.

"Have you thought about what you want to do?" I asked and then felt the need to clarify my words. "About us, I mean." I crossed my fingers without him knowing it - something I did a lot as a child.

"I don't want this to end," he assured me.

Those were the words I needed to hear and I silently sighed. Aaron slipped his arms around me, drew my body close and kissed my neck.

"I'll write you whenever I can and at the times I can't write, I'll try to call you."

"You promise?" I asked leaning back to scan his face.

"Of course, I promise," he replied squeezing me tighter. "I'm not at all happy about leaving you and wish more than ever that I was stationed closer to you. All I can do right now is promise to write."

As noted before, I had a thousand facial expressions that I could not hide. When Aaron saw my solemn look, he seemed nervous.

"You will write me back, won't you?" he asked.

"Of course, my love." I smiled hoping to erase his concern.

When we returned to my house, he walked me to the front door and pulled me close. We kissed passionately, both knowing that the following year would likely be the longest one of our lives. I tried to be strong and imprinted this moment in my mind so it would never be forgotten.

"I wish I never joined the army," he whispered in my ear.

"I know," I replied feeling a shiver overtake me.

We stood holding each other not wanting to let go. Aaron's hands caressed my back as he held me tight. It was a little awkward because neither of us wanted to say goodbye first.

"I should probably be going," he said finally in a low tone.

I did not want to hear those words but knew they were inevitable. I nodded and began to cry, no longer able to control my tears. I felt a knot form in my chest making it hard to breathe. Aaron drew away from me lifting my chin with his hand.

"I will write you," he promised again, his eyes focused lovingly on mine.

Saying goodbye was much harder than I imagined.

"Okay," I replied resignedly.

Then he kissed me softly one last time. I watched his back as he took a couple of steps away from me. In a panic, I called to him.

"Aaron, I almost forgot something!"

I quickly ran into the house leaving him looking confused. Sitting on my dresser was the letter I wrote the night before. I picked it up and began to cry. This really was goodbye. Wiping the tears away, I returned outside and handed him the letter.

"My address is written inside. Please write to me soon so I can write you back."

I hugged Aaron almost in desperation. "It scares me that you're going to be a soldier," I sobbed, tears streaming down my face. Now out of control, my body trembled. I could already feel the pain of his absence and reacted without thinking.

"I'll be okay," Aaron assured as he opened his arms enfolding me within them.

He held me for a long time and ended the embrace with a heartfelt kiss. Then he slipped from my arms and strolled back to his car.

"Do me a favor?" I pleaded as he reached his car. "Don't read my letter until you're on the plane?"

Aaron nodded and still unable to control my distress, I ran after him. I just had to kiss him one more time before he got behind the wheel. I took a step backward as the car slowly began to roll. The window was down and he waved back at me.

"Say hello to your dad for me… and remember… I love you," I cried as he drove away.

I stood in the street watching until it he drove out of sight. I returned to the house and made my way to my bedroom – nearly blinded by tears. I did not know what the future held for me but I did know I wanted Aaron to be a part of it. I already wanted him back with me - where he was meant to be.

Later that evening when my roommates returned home, they attempted to console me. I relived our last couple of days, telling them of our adventures during our

time together. I could almost feel Aaron's hand in mine as I shared each memory.

As the days passed, I found myself laughing over some of the silly things Aaron did such as when we went fishing and he fell into the water. Over the next couple of weeks, Zack's teasing reappeared.

"Now that the cat's away the mice can play," he joked. I wondered if Aaron was right about him.

It took three weeks before I finally received my first letter from Aaron. I was so excited just holding the envelope and clutching it to my heart. A few tears escaped before I opened it and sucked in a breath. Blinking tears from my eyes, I read his letter.

Aaron noted his day started at 5 a.m. and that he had to be in formation by 5:30. The unit ate breakfast at 6:30 a.m. and then took part in the day's training from 8:30 a.m. until 12 p.m. Lunchtime was promptly at noon and more training followed from 1 to 5 p.m. I tried to imagine him doing pushups and jumping jacks, which helped put a smile on my face.

From 6 to 8:30 p.m., the drill sergeant took over leaving Aaron only one hour of personal time before lights out. He noted that members of his unit became best friends with M16's, as well as machine guns and a grenade launcher, just to name a few. I already knew he loved guns, so assumed that this part of the training would be easy for him.

He also wrote that physical activities included tackling obstacles over 40 feet high, as well as hand-to-hand combat. As I recalled him flexing his arm, I could not

help smiling. He also noted that he had to enter a gas chamber, which he was less than thrilled about. Then he ended the letter by relating how he missed me terribly and hoped I would still wait for him.

"I miss you too, Aaron," I whispered carefully folding his letter and sliding it back in the envelope.

I was so thrilled to finally receive a letter from him and even more so, that I had an address to write him back. After sharing the news with my roommates, I quickly pulled out my scented stationary. First of all, I let Aaron know how things were going at the beauty salon and how my business had picked up. I wrote about my daily routine as well as how empty my life felt without him. Of course, I also told him how badly I missed him too. I noted that he might have been right about Zack but not to worry, that he was the one I loved and only he held the key to my heart. As before, I put on some lipstick and kissed the back of the envelope.

That night, I fell asleep much easier than I had in a long time with pleasant dreams of Aaron and I that seemed so real. I awoke in a fantastic mood and could not wait to share everything Aaron wrote with the girls at the beauty salon.

Chapter 15
Disaster Strikes

Who knew that the morning of April 19, 1995 would change my life forever? My first customer arrived at 8 a.m. and was soon under the hairdryer with another client in for a shampoo and set sitting in my chair. Of course, I shared my excitement over the letter from Aaron while I worked.

It was a sunny day outside with a calm and blissful sky. No one could have imagined what was about to happen. It was a couple of minutes after 9 a.m. when we felt the building shake. Being in a beauty salon - gossip central - everyone had an opinion on what might be happening. Betty was sure it was an earthquake but before she could even defend her theory, Carol called out shrilly and pointed to the television. None of us were prepared for what we saw.

Someone had just bombed the Alfred P. Murrah Federal Building in downtown Oklahoma City. As we listened, we learned that a man had left an explosive-filled truck in front of the building. We all stood staring at the TV not sure we really understood what we just heard. This terrorist act happened just a few miles away from us and it left us stunned. Carol cried aloud saying she knew people who worked in the Murrah Building. She ran to the phone and began calling to see if they were all right. Veronica's eyes remained glued to the TV like a zombie.

As for me, I felt a tremendous urge to go to the site to see if I could help in some way. I was not quite sure how or why I felt that way but knew I needed to be there. My body flinched and a kind of energy formed inside me that I did not understand. I felt anxious and could not divert my attention to anything else, especially not my work. It was amazing how something like this could take control of the mind to the exclusion of everything else.

I managed to finish with my two clients and called the rest of my customers to let them know I would be out for the rest of the day. I had to get to Oklahoma City as quickly as possible. I was not sure where to go but my boss gave me directions and I drove off. On the way, I was so anguished by this event that I had trouble catching my breath and tears blurred my vision. Somehow, I finally I found the site of the devastation.

Members of the National Guard were everywhere with rifles in hand. The area resembled a war zone. Having lived in Lawton my entire life, I should have been used to seeing these uniforms but it frightened me when I saw the heavily armed men. Two of them waved their hands to stop my car. They walked to each side of the vehicle and asked me where I thought I was going.

"I just want to help?" I cried my head swiveling as I tried to look at both of them.

They glanced inside my car inspecting the contents before they pointed in the direction I should go to park. I then hurried along a couple of blocks on foot before arriving at the outskirts of what they called the State Emergency Operations Center. As I climbed the cement steps leading up to it, my legs wobbled and became weak from the nervousness within my body. Even so, I pressed on using every ounce of strength I could muster.

A uniformed gentleman stood at the door, his stern eyes examining me before he spoke.

"What can I do for you," he asked in a firm yet polite tone. His expression was hard with no smile on his face or in his eyes.

Does he think I'm the enemy, I wondered as tears fell again.

"I want to help?" I pleaded in an almost fearful voice.

"Do you have any identification?" he asked.

He extended one hand while the other firmly held his rifle. I took out my driver's license and he quickly scanned the information written on it.

"Do you have anything to show me that you're medical personnel?" he asked handing the license back to me.

"What?" I squeaked. I was confused. I had come to help in any way I could because I felt compelled to be there. This compulsion was not just a request but also a command made by my body, mind and soul.

"I used to be a life guard and I know CPR..."

The man instantly cut me off by throwing his hand, palm forward, up in the air and would not let me finish. His actions caused me to jump backward.

"Go on home," he barked. "We're only allowing doctors and nurses to pass." Then he motioned to show me the way to leave. I could not believe what I heard and tried to assure him that I could be of assistance.

"But I can hold someone's hand or stop someone's bleeding," I noted.

He continued to stand formally with a straight and stern face.

"Go home," he repeated, his brows rising up to meet his nose. "We can't use you."

This scared me even more and I knew not to argue any further. I ran down the stairs, almost tripping before I reached the bottom. Then I dropped onto the last step and sobbed. Never in my life had I felt so helpless. When I reached my car and drove past the National Guard again, it seemed as difficult to get by going out as it did getting in. Then I hit the gas pedal and sped home.

When I arrived, I found my roommates sitting in the living room together in front of the television. Lynn and Jessica were out of school that day because they closed the college after the bombing occurred. I slumped on the couch, eyes red, and my face swollen and streaked from my tears. Lynn tried to comfort me with a hug but she could not help crying too.

The news stated that a Ryder Truck was found in front of the north side of the Murrah Federal Building. It was assumed that hundreds of people were killed and/or injured.

"We don't have the exact toll yet but will let you know when we do you," the announcer noted. "This bombing has damaged buildings in a sixteen-block radius leaving hundreds of people homeless and multiple offices shut down today in Oklahoma City. Fire fighters, ambulance and police arrived at the scene once they heard the blast. Within the first hour, many people were rescued and sent to nearby hospitals but rescue efforts are being

suspended due to fears that there could be a second bomb."

I felt a mixture of emotions including uselessness and helplessness. All I wanted was to help somehow, to do anything to assist the victims. My heart ached in my chest and I had trouble catching my breath as I continued to cry with the other girls.

"I can't believe we had a terrorist attack right here in Oklahoma," said Zack shaking his fist. His face was flush with anger and looked as if he might take a swing at something.

"I think it's from Islamic terrorists," Jim interjected. "Remember the World Trade Center bombing in 1993? I think they're at it again."

The boys continued to hypothesize about the attack while we girls sat holding each other.

Then the TV caught our attention again: "The rescue efforts have resumed with the removal of what they think might be the second bomb."

How could this really be happening? I wondered.

We watched as the news portrayed the devastation. An aerial view panned the building, which showed one side of it missing like someone sheered it off. We could see the open floors with desks, chairs and papers fluttering down. The ground outside was covered with bricks, construction material and debris. Black smoke and ash covered the skyline and land around the area. Cars in the parking lot were damaged and smoking. We heard sirens blaring and people yelling. Many ran down the street crying, dirty and bleeding.

The news report also showed firefighters trying to pull people out of the destruction. Some carrying babies covered in blood while others struggled to carry bleeding adults. The newscaster stated that one-third of the building was blown away and that this horrible event mimicked the end of the world. At 4 p.m., President Bill Clinton spoke to the nation and declared a federal state of emergency.

"The bombing in Oklahoma City was an attack on innocent children and defenseless citizens," he said. "It was an act of cowardice and it was evil. The United States will not tolerate it and I will not allow the people of this country to be intimidated by evil cowards."

That night I wrote to Aaron to tell him about the bombing and how much I wished he were home. I told him how I traveled to the city hoping to help but was turned away feeling helpless and defeated. I expressed how much I needed his arms wrapped around me for comfort but would have to be satisfied with our memories. Ending the letter, I wrote of my undying love for him and that I hoped to hear from him again soon. When I was done, I laid on my bed staring at the ceiling, my mind still preoccupied with replaying the day's horrible event and wondering what else I could possibly do to help. Little did I know that this day would instill a new desire in my heart and lead me toward a totally unexpected future.

Chapter 16
A Surprise Visit

At work the following morning, news of the bombing replaced the usual gossip. We learned that one hundred and sixty-eight lives were lost, including nineteen children, and six hundred and eighty were injured. My heart ached as I listened to the discussion growing more and more anxious.

Then one of my customers lit an unexpected fire under me when she noted that she was an instructor at The Moore-Norman Vo-Tech. She added that some of her students who were training to be emergency medical technicians (EMTs) were involved in clinical work and experienced firsthand how to help during a disaster.

I was intrigued and realized at that moment that I had to follow the same route. The very next day, I made an appointment to talk with a counselor to learn what this would entail. I took the pre-tests and was accepted for EMT-B class. Although I was not sure what I was getting myself into, I knew in my heart that I was meant to help others in this way.

Aaron wrote to tell me how he was doing in basic training. He already went through the gas chamber and wrote, he never wanted to experience that again. He also related that his unit learned to march in formation as well as how to quickly take apart and put together a weapon. He revealed how helpless he felt over not being home with me when the bombing occurred but was grateful that I was all right. He knew I was a strong person and loved the side of me that wanted to help. He

then reminded me of how I helped him and his dad talk again after the death of his mother. Finally, he wrote of how much he missed me and that my picture kept him going. He ended with, "My love to you forever."

Over the next few months, I became preoccupied with my new goal. I wrote Aaron to tell him about the school where I enrolled so I could work as an EMT with ambulance personnel. I explained that after I passed the course, I could be a first responder on a scene like the Oklahoma bombing to stabilize the victims before transporting them to a hospital. I hoped he understood how important this new direction in my life was to me and that he could share my excitement. I had finally found my purpose in life. I ended my letter with, "My love always."

As usual, I wrote on scented paper and put on lipstick to kiss the back of the envelope to show my love. Our letters were constant and I enjoyed reading them as much as writing them.

By July, Aaron graduated from basic training. I felt both excitement and depression over this because I could not be there to see him. I was already taking the EMT classes but when he called, I told him how proud I was of him. He had AIT to go to and would be gone for fourteen more weeks of training. He said he would be training for field artillery and was not yet sure where he would be sent.

One Friday afternoon while working at the beauty salon, I received a wonderful surprise. I was sitting at my station reading when a uniformed man walked in. He strode right up to me and asked for a haircut. I

recognized his voice but he looked much different than he had before. His beautiful long hair was gone leaving only a halo of black around his scalp.

"Excuse me," he said with his smile that showed the dimples I loved. "Do you have time to give me a haircut?"

I jumped from my chair and fell into Aaron's arms. Forgetting where we were, we embraced and our kiss lasted a couple of minutes. The girls at the salon started clapping, which embarrassed me… and helped to cut our kiss short.

"Have a seat stranger," I said gleefully when our lips parted. "I missed you so much."

"I missed you to," he replied smiling broadly.

His hand traced my jaw from my ear to my chin before he sat down. There was no need to shampoo his hair because he did not have much. I put a number one guard on my razor and planted it on his head leaving a slight stain of color around his scalp. When finished, Aaron rose from the chair looking so handsome in his army uniform.

"Why didn't you tell me you were in town?" I asked. "I would have picked you up at the airport."

His eyes stared lovingly into mine but his face reflected the weariness of his last few weeks of training.

"Do you have any plans?" he asked ignoring my question. "Are you hungry?" It was a question I'd heard often before he left.

"Always," I responded taking his hands in mine and not letting my eyes stray from his still handsome face.

"Come on, I know a good sandwich shop here in town," he chuckled.

After making sure I had no more customers, I told Carol that I quit for the day. We left the beauty salon and walked to the deli down the strip. When we entered, the middle-aged woman behind the counter almost fell over; she was so surprised. Once we sat down to eat, we discussed what had been happening in our respective lives.

Aaron told me his dad picked him up from the airport so he could have his own car to ride back to Lawton. He would be going to Fort Sill for his AIT and learning about cannons. That frightened me somewhat but I did not want to show my fear. He said his unit would only get a few twenty-four hour leaves during the next six months and only for good behavior so I probably would not see him much.

Then he announced that he had a surprise for me. He had a couple of days to spend with me before he had to return to Fort Sill. My heart jumped for joy when I realized he would be closer to home. At least during the few times he could leave the base, I would be able to drive down, stay at my parent's home and enjoy some time with him.

When we finished eating and headed for the door, Aaron stopped to promise Thelma that he would come back to visit her one more time before he left again. We rode to the park with the ducks but instead of feeding them this time, we made out in his car like two love-crazed teenagers. The touch of his skin felt so good, as his arms encircled me, holding and kissing me again. My

love for Aaron had grown even more since the last time I saw him.

What they say about distance making the heart grow fonder must be true, I thought.

We drove to Shawnee where his dad had supper waiting for us. We again talked about Aaron when he was growing up. Aaron energetically shared some of what he would learn at AIT. My stomach ached as I listened because those new skills sounded much more dangerous.

Aaron asked me to stay the night at his dad's house promising to have me home early in the morning for work. If he had given me a heads up about this visit, I could have taken the day off but I had already scheduled a full day of customers. However, I wanted to squeeze in as much time as I could with him and accepted. I was given the guest room and his dad offered a nightgown that once belonging to his wife.

After saying goodnight to the boys, I jumped into bed and stared at the ceiling. It was difficult to sleep knowing Aaron was in the next room. A little while later and after I had finally fallen asleep, I awoke when the bedroom door squeaked open. Wearing boxer shorts and an undershirt, Aaron tiptoed quietly into the room.

"Shh," he said with one finger to his lips.

He climbed in bed next to me, put his arms around me, and we kissed and giggled for most of the night. It felt so good to feel his body against mine. Finally, he slipped out of the bed and returned to his room so I could get a little sleep before arising for work in the morning.

The smell of breakfast woke me up and I hurried to get dressed. In the kitchen with a cup of coffee and two warm eggs in front of me, I listened to Aaron's plans for the day with his father. They were going to our fishing spot but would be shooting clay pigeons. I felt like I was missing out because of work but I also understood that Aaron needed to share some time with his father.

After thanking his dad for the wonderful meal and saying goodbye, Aaron drove me to work in Norman. The sun, which was slowly climbing in the morning sky, blinded us making it difficult to see the road. Nevertheless, we arrived safely and with a kiss goodbye, he told me he would see me later that night. With an ache in my heart, I watched him drive away.

The day seemed to drag on and if it weren't for all the customers, it might have felt like the longest day in history. Finally at 6 p.m., I finished with my last customer. Aaron sat outside in the parking lot waiting for me like he promised. He took me to a little Italian restaurant for dinner and then drove to the duck pond. As we sat in the car, he told me that he had to be back on base at 6 a.m. Tuesday morning. I went home smiling that night and could not wait to see him again the following day.

It was a Sunday, so we went to church with Jessica and Lynn in toe. Afterward, we returned to the house and plopped onto the couch. Zack and Jim were watching a baseball game. Somehow, the conversation drifted from army life to the Oklahoma bombing. Aaron left that night with a passionate kiss goodbye and a promise to be back early the next day.

Chapter 17
The Green-Eyed Monster

Monday began the way I hoped. I already had the coffee brewing when Aaron showed up with bagels. My mom called and I let Aaron say a few words to her. When I spoke with her, I said I would call her next week after he left. I was elated because he promised to come to school with me that day. We went to Subway for lunch and finally at 5 p.m., we walked into my class.

I could feel the tension build in Aaron's hand as he scanned the room. There was only one girl in the class and ten boys. His face reflected his concern but I tried to ignore it. After all, he had nothing to worry about. I loved him.

My teacher accepted Aaron sitting and watching, especially since he wore his uniform. Everyone greeted him politely and thanked him for his army participation, especially after going through the recent bombing. We were working on our practical training, which would be included on the exams coming up in the next few weeks. The class practiced patient assessment on a long board with me as the patient.

Four fellows played the part of the emergency medical technicians on scene. As I lay on the floor, the teacher explained the scenario. I had been in a car accident and was found lying on the street unconsciousness.

"Someone has just called 911," she said. "What do you do now?"

"We have arrived on the scene," said a fellow wearing a blue shirt looking a little confused. "We have to make sure the scene is safe first?"

"Good," she replied. "Go on."

"We put on our gloves," he said with a faint smile. As he did so, he nodded to the other fellows who followed his lead.

"We make sure the scene is safe," he repeated. "Then we approach the patient."

He moved slowly to my side and looked down at me. I sensed his confusion as he tried to remember what he was supposes to do. Meanwhile, I had to lie straight but I moved my eyeballs so I could squint at Aaron. I could see him trying not to smile as the blue-shirted fellow awkwardly tried to get through the procedure.

"Now what do you do?" asked the teacher with some irritation, drumming her fingers impatiently on her desk.

"I call my team to help."

He glanced at the other fellows and motioned for them to assist him. They moved next to me carrying a backboard. Placing the board on the floor beside me, the one in blue got down to his knees to hold my head and neck with his hands. The other three got on their knees - one by my back, one by my buttocks and one by my legs. The one in blue counted to three before they rolled my body over to place me on the backboard. I peeked over to Aaron, who seemed antsy in his seat.

"Good job, boys. Now what's next," the instructor coaxed.

One of the guys wearing yellow scooted on his knees toward my face and glided his fingers around my skull to

ensure nothing was broken. The first fellow knelt by my head and kept his hands on my neck and cheeks. The one in yellow touched my face, and slid his fingers around my nose and cheeks.

"Airway clear," he yelled. His fingers then moved to my throat and the top of my chest. Clumsily feeling the bones of my upper ribs, he tried to avoid my breasts.

"No crepitus," he yelled, meaning no cracking or grating feeling under the skin. The ribs were not fractured and moving.

At this point, it sounded like someone slammed a foot to the ground and I wondered if it was Aaron. Next the fellow slid his hands toward my belly - one hand over the other, pushing down and palpating around.

"Soft with no tenderness," he said loudly.

The other two boys remained on their knees watching and learning. I heard a chair move, which got my attention and saw Aaron stand up. His eyebrows down over his nose, his face scowled. The teacher seemed to ignore the interruption and kept her eyes on the students. The guy in yellow placed his hands on each side of my hips and pushed inward.

"No broken pelvis."

Then I heard stamping footsteps moving toward the classroom door. The fellow in yellow placed one hand on top of my thigh and one at the back of my thigh, and started squeezing my leg all the way down to my feet. With this, Aaron stomped out of the room and slammed the door. I finished my class without him.

Afterward, I ran to the parking lot looking for him. He was standing next to one of the building's brick walls with one foot resting on it, his knee bent backwards. Quietly, I approached him.

"Hi." I said forcing a smile.

Aaron just nodded and looked at the ground.

"What's wrong?" I asked.

"Nothing," he said, an obvious lie.

I walked around him trying to get him to look at me but he completely ignored me. I did have a temper even though I'd never shown it to him. I grew angry at his silent treatment and threw up my hands.

"What's this all about, Aaron? I had to apologize to my class for your behavior and I don't even understand what's wrong."

"I'm mad," he finally admitted.

"Duh, no kidding, Sherlock… but why?"

He shrugged his shoulders still not letting his eyes meet mine. I assumed he must be jealous.

"Give me an answer," I demanded. "I think I deserve that much." Raising my voice I added, "You were just plain rude - a side of you I've never seen before."

"Well it's your fault…"

"My fault? Oh no! Don't blame this on me. I didn't do anything wrong." I crossed my arms indignantly waiting for an answer. Aaron stalled for a few minutes before finally speaking.

"I'm sorry," he mumbled shifting from one foot to the other.

"I want to know what's bothering you," I pressed.

We stood staring at the ground or up at the sky but not at each other. I finally put my back against the wall and leaned my head back with my eyes closed. I did not understand Aaron's reaction but I did know that I only had that night before he would be leaving. I would not see him again for a few weeks and could not let our time together end this way.

"Come with me," I begged grabbing his arm.

Half willingly, he followed me to his car.

"Let me drive."

Aaron dropped into the passenger seat, still moping. He did not ask where I was taking him. He just stared out the window quietly. Finally, I arrived at the place I wanted to show him. He followed me out of the car to a barbed wired fence. Our eyes peered through the fence showing the destruction of the Oklahoma bombing. The building and surrounding area was still covered with debris from the blast. Aaron's face conveyed anxiety as he surveyed the site.

Then we walked around the block to view all the pictures, flowers and stuffed animals left in memory of the adults and children who lost their lives. I put my arm around him and spoke softly.

"This is why I'm becoming an EMT. Look around and see the devastation." Tears formed in my eyes just as they did the day of the bombing and saw this site for the first time. "I want you to understand why I'm doing what I'm doing. I want to help. Just like you're helping our country by being in the army, I want to help people in this city." I felt his arm encircle my waist.

"I'm sorry, Annette," he sighed. "Now put yourself in my shoes. I haven't seen my girl in a long time and then I go to her class consisting mostly of boys and watch them touch her body. I know what they were thinking while they held your head or touched you. You are beautiful and of course, they want more. Plus now they know your boyfriend's in the army, they'll think they have a chance with you."

I broke down in tears. Some of them were for the reminder of the destruction in front of me and some were for Aaron. How could he not know how much I love him? I wondered.

He held my body closely as I trembled and kissed me a couple of times. We stood silently as the sun went down. Finally, he whispered that it was time to take me home.

We drove up to my house to find the lights out so we entered quietly and crept to my room. I sat on the bed patting it to indicate he should sit next to me. He held me tight before he leaned in for a kiss and somehow this one seemed different, more vibrant and alive. My body responded to his kiss and touch as he slowly slipped off my shirt. My breathing grew short and rapid. I did not want him to stop.

Aaron removed his shirt and as he moved closer, I felt his warm chest against mine. He kissed my cheek and slid his tongue to my neck before exploring my chest. We took off the rest of our clothes and the sensation of his body against mine felt like fire. Then we made passionate love. When we finished, he stayed beside me, his arms wrapped around me.

"I love you so much," he whispered.

It would have been easy for me to fall asleep while he held me gently but I knew Aaron had to get up at 3 a.m. to leave for Fort Sill. As he stood by my bed in the early hour, he looked so impressive in his uniform. With the touch of his hand and the taste of his lips one last time, he said I had nothing to worry about, that we would survive this absence from each other. I had never made love to a man before, nor had I ever loved anyone like I love Aaron. I hoped he realized that I had given him not just my heart but also my essence the element of my being. After he left, I cried myself to sleep once more.

Chapter 18
Real Life Emergency

The next couple of months flew by quickly as I continued my EMT course. I discovered a new and exciting world learning about such things as how to take vitals, and use a blood pressure cup and stethoscope. I learned that the numbers from the cuff and stethoscope represented the pressure against the walls of a person's blood vessels as the blood moved through. The systolic pressure occurred when the heart contracted. The diastolic pressure occurred when the heart relaxed. Normal blood pressure was around 120 (systolic) over 80 (diastolic), which was written as 120/80 mmHg.

There was not much I could do if the patient had high blood pressure when the systolic was over 140 and the diastolic was over 90 but if the blood pressure fell low - the systolic under 90 - then I could take action. I would lay the patient down and lift the person's legs to help the blood pressure to rise. I was taught that this was a hypotensive state.

I also learned that low blood pressure could cause dizziness, fainting and even serious heart, endocrine and neurological disorders but most important was that low blood pressure could deprive the brain of oxygen possibly throwing the patient into shock or even a life-threatening situation. It might sound strange but the words 'life threatening' actually excited me. I felt like this was my destiny, to help someone in a life-threatening situation.

I attended school two nights a week and still worked with plenty of time to study as well as spend some time

with my roommates. Aaron and I still wrote letters telling each other what we were doing with our time. Aaron tried to explain his Military Occupation Specialty (MOS or his job in the army). His position was called 'cannon crewmember' so his MOS was 13B. He was being taught to operate a high technology cannon artillery weapon system. He learned to load and fire howitzers along with setting fuses to high explosive artillery rounds, scatterable mines and rocket-assisted projectiles. He participated in security operations and position preparations. I was not sure what that meant but I did not like the sound of it. In fact, it seemed far too dangerous.

Sometimes he worked all night using night vision devices in camouflage positions. He also learned critical combat survival skills that he could use in a hostile environment. He ended the letter by telling me he was safe and not to worry about him. He said he often looked at my picture to help him keep going and he loved me more than life itself.

By then, I started my clinical on an ambulance with real EMT's, so I wrote primarily of my experiences. I told him how thrilling it was to race along with the lights and sirens blaring. I also noted how scary it was when other cars just stop in front of us or would not move to the right. A couple of times, the ambulance driver had to veer to the opposite side of the road with cars coming straight at us. My heart never beat so fast as I watched the headlights rushing our way! Fortunately, they eventually moved aside so we could drive through.

I also told Aaron about a call we received for someone wanting to commit suicide at 2 a.m. It looked like something out of a movie as I walked up the stairs of the motel with the two fellows who were training me. Police were gathered on the steps and on the walkway toward the motel room. It was dark with only the lights above the doors to help us see where we were going. The door was open with a dim light emanating from a lamp inside and I could see a couple of officers.

When we entered the room, the bed was to the right of us with the sheets covered in blood. To the left was a dresser with a television sitting on it. Straight ahead was the bathroom. The room was messy with food wrappers on the floor. I grew more and more apprehensive but hoped my anxiety did not show. The paramedic walked over to one of the officers and they whispered to each other. My eyes shot to the bathroom door when I heard someone yell.

"Hey," a man yelled from inside. "Go away."

"I tried to talk to him but he refused to come out," said one of the police officers. "I know how to get him out but I want you guys here in case we needed you."

The paramedic nodded and urged the man to listen.

"Come on out," he said as he jiggled the door handle.

I learned that after the police received this call about a person who planned to kill himself, they arrived to find the bathroom door locked. The man had secluded himself inside and they wanted to bust it open but called us when they saw the blood on the bed and could not coax him out.

"There seems to be a lot of blood on the bed," the paramedic continued. "Are you hurt? Let me look at you to see if I can bandage you up."

All was quiet at first as we waited to see what the man would do but all of a sudden, we heard the shower running.

"Go away," muffled the man. "I want to die."

One of the police officers knocked on the bathroom door.

"Come on out, young man," he said scowling and looking agitated. "You three need to go outside," he added taking something out of his pocket. I did not ask any questions and did as I was told.

"I will give you until the count of three before I let off this tear gas," he hollered. We immediately ran from the room.

"You can't do that," shouted the voice on the other side. "That's police brutality!"

"Don't you know it's against the law to commit suicide?" the officer noted trying to maintain his patience.

"Just let me die," the man wailed.

"One," said the officer holding out the can in his hand. Another officer handed him a gas mask.

"Two."

Three officers stayed in the motel room with masks on and the rest joined us outside.

"Please," the man pleaded. "I just want to die. Let me do it in peace."

"Three!" The officer yelled and ripped opened the can.

Tear gas quickly flooded the room and it only took seconds before the bathroom door swung open. A tall young man with long wet hair hanging around his face and down his shoulders stumbled out. Blinded by the gas, he complained that his eyes burned. He was naked, blood dripping from both wrists tracing the length of his arms. The shower was still running. It seemed he stood in it hoping the hot water would help him bleed faster. After wrapping a coat around him, the police escorted the man outside. We then stepped in and wrapped his arms with gauze before assisting him down the stairs to an awaiting gurney. We then transferred him so we could drive him to the hospital. I was able to check his vitals, playing with the things I learned in class. This was all so exhilarating.

I ended my letter with, "My love forever, Annette."

Chapter 19
Relationship By Letters

Finally November 1995 rolled around and I was going to graduate from the EMT-B course. Aaron was graduating from his advanced individual training but wanted to move up in the skill levels in hopes of reaching cannon crewmember. I tried to be happy for him and hoped to hide my sorrow. I did not want him in such a dangerous situation as a cannon crewmember might experience. Meanwhile, I went on to EMT–I class - a prerequisite to work my way up to being a full-fledged paramedic.

Before either of us began our new adventures, we both had a week off so I drove to Fort Sill to meet Aaron. He looked so handsome in his uniform. Although I still missed his long black hair, his body was in tip-top shape with his muscles bulging through his uniform. He smiled showing his dimples and I fell in love all over again.

He got in the car and leaned over to give me a kiss. Then we drove to my parent's home so he could finally meet them. When he walked into the house, my mom surprised him with a hug hello. The crock-pot was on and she informed us that we would be having beef stew for dinner. After saying hello to my dad, we left the house and I showed him around Lawton. This quiet town had a small shopping mall and its own duck pond. I had bread in the car so we walked around the park feeding the ducks. As we did, we talked about our days apart and what we had been doing.

That night after dinner with my folks, the boys sat down to watch sports on television. Mom and I washed the dishes and cleaned up the kitchen. My folks did not have a guest room so I threw some sheets on the couch for Aaron but in the middle of the night, I snuck out of my room and tiptoed into the living room. I just wanted to hold him for a few minutes without getting caught. Lying on the couch together, we kissed and hugged for some time. There was something romantic and exciting about being sneaky like that.

The following day, we drove to Mount Scott to hike on a new trail. We spent one day at Fort Sill where he showed me the campus and another playing cards with my folks. We kept so busy and enjoyed each other's company so much that the week just flew by. Before we knew it, Aaron had to leave for Fort Sill, while I had to return to Norman to start EMT-I. As before we said goodbye, which hurt my heart all over again.

I started my new class and the joy of learning new things took over. I reviewed the skills I had already learned including patient assessment and management, ventilatory management, spinal immobilization and bleeding control. Then I learned how to put intravenous into people's arms and administer D-50, which was sugar given when someone had a blood sugar count under 60. I was like a wet sponge just soaking in all the new information and skills.

A few weeks later, I received a letter from Aaron. He was supervising an operation, and loading and maintaining a field artillery support vehicle. He achieved

a higher rank at E-3 and wanted to become a specialist or E-4. Judging by the words he wrote, it seemed that he had decided to make the army his career.

A couple of months went by and Aaron was granted some 24-hour leaves. When these occurred, he drove to Norman to visit me, as well as Shawnee to see his dad. I was only able to be with him for an occasional walk or perhaps dinner and then he returned to Lawton. I stayed busy riding along with an ambulance and doing my clinical work in the hospital's emergency room.

It seemed as if school was making it impossible for me to visit with Aaron for any length of time. Due to the rising tension over our inability to be together as much, we sometimes argued. I know we both hated this but seemed powerless to stop it. I am sure he blamed me for the distance that was growing between us. Yet each time we experienced another tearful goodbye, we put the arguments aside. We really needed to spend more time alone together but I did not see that happening in the near future.

Following our last goodbye and his return to base, Aaron received some surprising news and wrote to tell me about it. I sat on my bed, imagining that he was with me as I read his letter. It was as if I could actually hear his voice. I also thought of those cute dimples that appeared like magic whenever he smiled.

Dear Annette,

I know we have been drifting apart. I also know it isn't your fault or mine but I also realize that what we have is wonderful and that we are trying to keep it alive. I am so sorry that we have been fighting lately and I want to reiterate that it's not your fault. I hope you to know that.

I have just received new orders and will be leaving this week for Afghanistan. My job is to help keep some semblance of order and to assist the civilians who live there. I won't sugar coat this for you. This will be a dangerous mission since there are some militants that do not want us there but one I am proud to do this job.

My orders mean I will be gone for a year or so. You know how the military is; they can change their mind anytime they want. Unfortunately, you will be getting this letter after I leave. They didn't give me much time to prepare and won't even let me see my dad before I go. I will write you again with the new address as soon as I can. For now, you can send your mail to my old one and in time, I should receive it.

Just remember that I love you and miss you very much. Please don't forget me.

Love always, Aaron

I reread Aaron's letter several time and sobbed uncontrollably. My worst fears were becoming reality. Too distraught to put on my pajamas, I curled into a ball on my bed and cried myself to sleep. When the bright morning sun woke me up, I found myself in yesterday's clothes with my face swollen and red. After a hot shower, I decided that it would be best to keep myself busy. I

planned to funnel all of my frustration and energy into my classes at school.

With new enthusiasm, I delved in. I found cardiac strips fascinating. Those small pieces of paper with the wavy lines looked so foreign to me and I wondered if I would ever understand them. I also learned how to interpret an electrocardiogram (ECG). I calculated the heart rate by counting the number of large squares between QRS complexes (deflections on ten ECG) and divided them into 300. A heart rate over 100 beats per minute was a disorder of the heart called Tachycardia and a rate under 60 beats per minute was Bradycardia, which could lead to insufficient oxygen to the brain and other organs.

The letters P-QRS-T, which represented the complete heart, beat in an ECG. The P-wave, describes the atrial contraction, the QRS complex describes the ventricular contraction and the T-wave describes the ventricular decontraction. This all describes how the heart works and quite interesting.

My classes still ran a couple of times a week with a requirement of more ride time with the ambulances and clinical time at the hospital. This class seemed harder than EMT- B and I needed to study more but I welcomed the challenge.

I wrote to Aaron and tried to sound positive despite my concerns. I really hoped he did not sense how frightened I was for him. I did not have his new address yet so I knew he would not get any of my letters for a

while. I had not heard from him and with each passing day, I missed him more.

At the beauty salon, Carol often turned on the news to keep up with military action in Afghanistan. The Taliban, who first promised to save the people, began committing large-scale massacres. Naturally, I worried that Aaron might run into them. The Islamic militant group tortured and hung their former president. I felt shivers up and down my spine wondering where my man was stationed and feared for his life.

I had a great imagination but also a morbid one. In my mind, I saw his troop walking through some business district surveying the people and trying to keep the peace. Then a sniper would start shooting at them or a child they thought was innocent would pull out a gun. This would be followed with the awful realization that they were forced to kill a child.

Finally, Aaron's first letter arrived but before reading it, I drove to the duck pond with some bread. Strolling around the pond, I threw out small pieces and relived our time together. His letter was in my pocket. When there was no more bread, I found a picnic table and sat down. Slowly, I took the envelope from my pocket and began reading. A gush of tears filled my eyes.

Dear Annette,

This is the first letter I have written since I got here. I haven't received any letters from you yet but I'm sure that all of a sudden, I will get a bunch at one time. The mail is not very dependable here. How are you? I want to start by telling you that I miss you with my body, mind and soul.

We landed in this God-forsaken place in mid-afternoon under a cloudless sky and were surrounded by sand. We were loaded immediately onto a bus and drove for hours until we arrived at probably the largest city of tents you could ever imagine. Believe it or not, we do have a PX, and the food is actually pretty good too.

We practice drills by day and take turns on watch by night. We hear rumors of enemy mortar fire but so far, they have all been false alarms. My squad will be leaving to an outlying neighborhood soon where we will move from house to house to clear the area of the enemy. While on patrol the other day in our convoy, we noticed a vehicle passing us driving crazily from side to side on the road. The man inside flagged us down. I got nervous and slid my weapon onto my lap to be ready for whatever came next. After we patted him down to make sure he wasn't wearing any bombs, we let him talk. He said there were bad people ahead of us. Sure enough just a few yards ahead, an IED (improvised explosive device, known as a roadside bomb) went off. Thank God, no one was hurt.

Afghanistan is not quite the way I thought it would be. Sand is everywhere and the wind can chill you to the bone at night. But I am happy to do my part to keep American safe.

I love you Annette and I can't wait to come home to you. You are the only reason I am able to do this job.

Love Always, Aaron

As before, I read the letter over and over. He was safe and he still loved me. Those were the words I needed to read most. Gasping for breath as the tears continued to flow; I tried to pull myself together so I could drive home. I needed to write him back immediately. I ran to my room, found the scented stationary and sat on my bed with pen in hand.

Dear Aaron,

I got your letter today and do you know what I did? I drove straight to the duck pond and threw bread into the water like we used to do. I could feel your hand in mine as I relieved our memories. Then I nursed some happy tears as I read your letter.

I am so glad I finally heard from you. I could hear your voice as my eyes read the words you wrote. I have been listening to the news, which frightens me terribly. I try to find out where you are and what you are going through. My imagination scares me even more. I pray every night that you will come home safely and will be counting the days until you are back in my arms.

I have been keeping myself busy with school. You have no idea how much more I have learned. I enjoy riding in the ambulance and doing my clinical at the hospital. My final testing will approach soon before I can finally go on to Paramedic school. This is getting a lot harder than I

thought but what else do I have to do with my time. I will make you proud. Please don't be a hero and keep your head low. Aaron, the night we made love I gave you my greatest gift I could give anyone. I hope you know that. I have never been with a man before and I gave you my love totally and without even a second thought that this was meant to be.

I love you Aaron. Please come home to me.
Love Forever, Annette

I put the letter in the envelope hoping the pretty scent would still linger until Aaron got it. As I did before, I kissed the back of the envelope with lipstick. Then I waited patiently for his next letter.

I finally graduated from the EMT – I class and then had to take the hardest one of all. I had talked to a lot of people who went to paramedic school, and heard their fears and worries over this course. It would involve intense training to make us efficient with patients in dynamic, chaotic and dangerous environments. We would learn how to react under stress, and to use compassion and care when moving a patient from one place to another. We would actually learn to save lives and the thought of it was enthralling. It was what I had hoped for since the Oklahoma bombing.

Our teaching entailed learning pediatric life support, CPR, defensive driving, pharmacology, cardiology, EMT systems management, disease control, first aid and advance life support. The paramedic classes would take ten months not including extra hours of clinical in the

emergency room, pediatrics and obstetrics, gynecology and time on the cardiac floor, as well as riding along in the ambulance with the fire department. There would be no life outside of school with classes, clinical and studying but I could not wait.

I wrote to tell Aaron about graduating and the passing grade I received. I also expressed my fears about the upcoming classes. We were not allowed to miss more than one quiz during the entire ten months. If I could not figure out something and missed two quizzes, I would have to start over from the beginning because this training involved life and death subjects. I was up for the challenge.

Chapter 20
A New Study Partner

In July 1996, I began paramedic school with great anticipation but I still had not received a letter from Aaron. Although my heart ached for him, I was overwhelmed with joy when I walked into the classroom. The first order of business was to get fitted for special shirts with the school logo on them. Then we settled in to learn about the roles and responsibilities of a paramedic. We had already gone over some of this in EMT-B and EMT-I but since I did not do this for a living yet, I needed all the review I could get. The teacher helped us understand lawsuits involving negligence. The four elements that must be proved were a duty to act, breach of duty, damage to the patient and breach, the proximate cause of damage. Wow, so much to learn!

We also talked about professional ethics and attitudes leading into the primary responsibility of a medic with how to prepare, respond and size up a scene. We discussed the initial patient assessment with treatment and management. Was this a play and stay patient meaning we would need to fix the life-threatening problem or was this a load and go patient, which meant we needed to get the patient to the hospital for a higher level of care. Last but not least, the teacher explained the importance of documenting our findings.

The class consisted of ten boys and five girls. I recognized a couple of students from some of the other classes but did not know most of them. It did not matter

though, because I was not there to make friends; I wanted to learn to save lives.

"Hey," said a boy sitting next to me during a break. "This is going to be intense, isn't it?"

I glanced over to him not really paying attention and shook my head.

"My name is Timothy Wright but everyone calls me Tim," he continued holding out his hand.

"Annette," I replied peeking up from under my bangs and shaking his hand.

"Have you gone over the syllabus?" he asked. "Looks like this is going to be a long year."

Detecting a little cockiness in his voice, I smiled to be polite and then turned away from him. However, I could still feel his stare. I rolled my eyes and despite my obvious lack of interest, he continued to talk.

"I plan to work with the fire department. My dad is a fire chief and I'm hoping to work on his crew," he noted but again I did not respond.

The month seemed prolonged with studies on the medical and legal aspects of pre-hospital care, and illness and injury prevention along with prevention strategies for motor vehicles, geriatrics and the workplace, just to name a few. I attended classes three nights a week and could not believe how co-operative my customers were as they worked around my schedule.

I was lucky enough to still have Monday mornings to myself and to enjoy my weekly phone conversations with mom but I did find myself sitting at Denny's Restaurant a couple of times a week studying so I would have no

interruptions. At home, I either got phone calls or my roommates pressed me to watch a movie with them. It seemed there was always something or someone that interfered with my studies. I did not want to let anything deter me from becoming a paramedic.

Listening to the television one day, a newscaster related how the Taliban took over some cites in Kabul and that the people were starving. They showed women and children in hospital with limbs missing either from accidentally stepping on a mine or because they were injured when caught stealing a piece of bread. I could not help crying. I immediately sat down and wrote to Aaron to let him know I was worried about him. I told him I hoped the reason I had not heard from him was due to the post office experiencing problems getting letters from the Middle East. I also wrote about school and what I was studying for the month. I let him know that I prayed for his safety every night and ended with: "I love you forever."

By August, I still had not received a letter from Aaron. However, school kept me busy as we learned to apply mathematical principals to real life medical situations using dosage calculations for intravenous, tablets, liquids and injectables. Okay, so math was not my best subject but I did enjoy the learning process and how I would use math to save lives.

I sat in class trying to figure out the volume of fluid to be infused, the period of time during which a fluid should be infused and the number of drops per milliliter the infusion set would deliver. Becoming a little frustrated, I set my pencil down and rubbed my temples.

"Can I help you?" asked Tim leaning over and smiling.

I could not help noticing a chip on one of his front teeth.

"Sure," I responded shrugging. Deep down, I was glad he wanted to help.

"It's like this," he said standing up.

I noticed that Tim was much taller than I originally thought. He picked up my pencil, took my paper and began writing.

"You take the volume to be infused times the drops/ml of infusion set divided by the total time of infusion in minutes."

He finished the calculation, lifted the pencil in the air and smiled showing all his teeth as if he was proud of himself.

"I still don't get it."

He looked at me as if I was stupid and did the calculation again. As it turned out, Tim was pretty good with math. He helped me as we went through the equivalents, metric, apothecary and household systems. He also showed me how to change pounds to kilograms to determine the correct dosage when administering drugs. After a couple of weeks, I got use to talking with and learning from him. We then moved to pharmacology, including how different medicines affected the human body. We had to memorize so many different drugs with their dosages and how they related to a person's weight.

I found myself studying more often at Denny's. One day, I heard footsteps approach and to my surprise, I saw

the smile with the chipped front tooth that I knew so well from school.

"Hi Annette," Tim said plopping into the seat across the booth from me. "I heard you say you studied here so I thought perhaps you might like a study partner." He waved down the waitress and asked for a Coke.

"Tim, what are you doing here?" I asked caught completely off guard. I'm afraid my voice sounded cold but the reason I studied at Denny's was to get away from the noise of my roommates and any interruptions that might distract me. I did not smile or even act happy to see him. I was on a quest to graduate and become a paramedic. That was all that mattered.

"To study," he said looking a little worried and clearly not understanding the tone of my voice.

"Tim, I plan on passing this class and I don't want anything or anyone to get in the way. I appreciate you helping me with my math but I'm serious. That's why I don't study at home."

I hoped he understood what I was trying to saying. I thought I made myself clear enough. I was not looking for a study partner or a boyfriend. My mind was only on school and waiting for Aaron to come home.

"Hey, missy," he jumped right back at me.

He actually scared me and my head flinched back. His eyes were hard and he appeared stiff necked as he continued.

"I have a lot riding on this too. My dad is as paramedic firefighter and I can't let him down." He closed his eyes and drew in a deep breath. Then I watched as he stood up.

Good, he has the right idea, I thought. I want to be left alone. I waited for him to walk away but he just stood and stared at me. He seemed to evaluate me before he spoke. I squinted figuring I must have made him angry.

"Look, I just want to study and I thought we could help each other," he said in a softer voice. His lips curved into a slight smile as he raised his hand across the table toward me. "Study partners… deal?"

I took a few seconds to reflect on what he said. He sounded serious and I actually believed him. I could sure use his help with math and if we could put all our energy on school, perhaps we could help each other. I raised my hand to meet his and a smile crept onto my face.

"Nothing else, correct?" I inquired making sure he understood the conditions of the deal. My eyes searched his face looking for anything untrustworthy but he seemed completely sincere.

"I am not looking for a boyfriend," I affirmed. "I am here to study and we are only study partners. Got it?"

"Partners," Tim said shaking his head in agreement. He sat back down and the waitress arrived with his Coke. He opened his book and was true to his word as we studied. We did not talk about ourselves but kept our conversation on the work at hand.

The following week was comprised entirely with work, school and Denny's to study with Tim. I wrote to Aaron again to tell him that school was becoming more difficult and most of the time, I was preoccupied with studying. I told him about my studies and how challenging I found the math because I was never that good with arithmetic. I

also noted that I had been a little too busy to watch television but sometimes at work my manager turned on the news. At those times, I tried to catch up on the Afghanistan war. To tell the truth, I found TV too hard to focus on because I was so worried about him and still needed to concentrate on school. I told him I was frightened because I had not heard from him and to please let me know if he was all right. I ended the letter with: "All my love, Annette."

I was unsure of how I felt about Aaron at that point. Part of me was angry because he did not write and another part was scared for his life. Sometimes I paced the floor of my room agitated and worried at the same time over receiving no letter or card from him. I wanted to believe that it was the mail's fault. I did not want to even consider that he might be hurt or even worse - that he had fallen out of love with me. I hurt inside when I re-read his past letters holding onto each word, wanting desperately to believe he still cared.

After my exhausting days I looked forward to sleep so I would not have to think anymore. I knew I had to be patient but it was becoming impossible. I looked forward to each new day and hoped that some news from Aaron would find its way to me.

Chapter 21
So Much to Learn

By September, there was still no letter but I continued to throw my all energy into school. I learned medical terminology, and attempted to understand medical abbreviations and acronyms. My teacher again explained the importance of documentation and ensuring that others could read and understand the story we built. If we did not write down what we did for the patient, then it would be assumed that a procedure was not done. That's when the legal aspect could come back to haunt you. In class, we also studied anatomy and physicality, memorizing all 206 bones of the body, not to mention remembering the names of all the muscles.

I was required to understand the skeletal, nervous, muscular, endocrine, cardiovascular, digestive, urogential (kidneys and reproductive), immune and respiratory systems. If that weren't enough, I also needed to understand the body's cellular structure and something called the Fick Principle, a technique for measuring cardiac output. As well, I learned about osmosis, diffusion and mediated transport mechanisms related to fluid replacement. Needless to say, I had little time for play anymore. I only went to work, school and Denny's, studying into the wee hours and even in my sleep. I could not take Monday's to myself anymore and sometimes, I even forgot what it was like to get a good night's sleep.

The waitress at Denny's got to know me, and what days and time I came in. They were so kind placing a

Coke on the table waiting for me. I was thankful that they let me sit in the restaurant for so many hours studying. Tim had become a regular study partner - our conversations staying, as promised, on school matters. We studied and quizzed each other, and to be honest, I surprised myself when I began to look forward to his company.

Since there was still no word from Aaron, I stopped writing as often. Of course, it was difficult to write to someone when no letters came back. It had been at least three months since I heard from him and my imagination worked overtime wondering why. I saw him hurt on the field or enjoying the attention of another girl who might share his interest in the military. I hated not knowing what was happening with him or where we stood.

Although I was hurt by his seeming lack of interest, I managed to get out a couple more letters to update him on my schooling and how uniquely the body worked. I explained that my life was completely consumed with school. I asked him to please write and added again that I was praying for his safety. I ended it with, "I love you, Annette."

October rolled around and again no letter. I felt like I was on an educational roller coaster because I ate, breathed and dreamed nothing but school. In class, we worked on airway and ventilation plus advanced life support. We learned about the respiratory system, and mastery of airway management and ventilation. I found it amazing how the body worked related to the mechanics of respiration. We also learned to intubate people, meaning we put a tube down their trachea and hooked

oxygen to it to help them breath, which was harder than it looked. We actually used a mannequin head that we put our metal blades into as we opened the mouth practicing to see the vocal cords so we could slide in an endotracheal tube. The most difficult part was trying to avoid touching the teeth. Funny thing was, these mannequin heads made a funny sound when we touched them.

We also reviewed CPR and practiced on each other to put in IV's. At the beauty salon, my customers teased me about shooting up because of all the bruises on my arms from the students missing my veins. As well, we learned to do intraosseous infusion, which meant putting a needle into a bone of the leg under the knee so medication could flow directly into the bone marrow. Of course, this was only done for life-threatening purposes and if we could not get an IV in. I found this most interesting.

Every month we were tested on our skills and knowledge, and required to keep a grade point average of at least 80 percent. Otherwise, we would be dropped from the class. I thanked my lucky stars and Tim that I was passing so far.

Near the end of the month when I returned home one evening from studying, my roommates announced that they planned to throw a Halloween party and asked me to join them.

"Come on," pleaded Lynn. "All you ever do anymore is study and work. You need to have fun sometimes."

"Have you heard from Aaron?" asked Jessica.

"No," I sighed aloud. My shoulders hung down along with my face showing my disappointment.

"You should stop moping around, girlfriend," Jessica said. "You need to meet some people and have a good time for a change." She stepped closer to me taking both my shoulders in her hands and giving them a small squeeze.

"Please," she begged as she searched my face for a positive response.

"Okay," I replied lifting my head to look at her and offering a faint smile.

Then Lynn shuffled over and both girls offered a group hug. I had not taken time for any fun since school started so I decided to take them up on their offer. Then I surprised myself when I broke my own rule by asking Tim to come to the party. His face lit up as he accepted the invitation.

On Halloween, my roommates decorated the house with hay on the floor, and witches and skeletons on the walls. The place was crawling with students. The laughter and music were so loud that we had to shout to carry on a conversation. I forgot how much fun it was to eat pizza and just relax. We played dunk for apples, mummy by wrapping a person in toilet paper and went on a scavenger hunt. Tim seemed to fit into the group after Lynn and Jessica grilled him. He looked so cute answering their questions and glancing at me every once in a while to give me a wink. Although we were busy with games and the party was so boisterous, I had a chance to enjoy Tim's company outside of school and Denny's for a change.

The following day, I decided to still write to Aaron despite the fact that I had not received anything from him. I miss him but honestly, I was so busy with school that I had placed him on the back burner. It was getting to the point where I could go a couple of days and not even think of him. During the day, I concentrated on school and at night, my dreams were filled with things like IV's and ECG monitors.

At the same time, Tim and I were falling into a comfortable and relaxed pattern. We continued to meet at Denny's to quiz each other and help each other pass at school. I expected to see that smile with the chipped tooth and on the days that he did not show up, I missed him. He seemed to be filling the void that Aaron left. I knew I still loved Aaron but how could I keep a relationship going with someone who did not communicate?

By November, I still received no mail from Aaron. In school, we were challenged with cardiac monitors, vents and glucose meters. We learned when to use the appropriate techniques to obtain someone's medical history and the pathophysiological significance – changes of normal mechanical, physical and/or biochemical functions - of a physical exam, as well as integrate the two to develop a process of clinical decision-making.

Wow, I had no idea how overwhelming this class would be. All the rumors I'd heard seemed to be right. I did not have a life anymore but school was destined to change it forever.

I was excited to start rotations but the hard part would be working them around my patron's hairstyling needs.

Fortunately, they were patient with me about the changed appointment times when I had to do something for school and sometimes even helped me study. I actually placed index cards around the mirror at my station and they quizzed me as I fix their hair. Nevertheless, I was afraid my rotations would consume too much of my work time since my bills still had to be paid.

November was the month that began the holidays and my mother loved cooking during this time. She called to find out if I would be home for Thanksgiving on Thursday but to her disappointment, I had to inform her that I was required to work a clinical in the emergency room that night and early the following day. This was not by choice. I also had customers' hair to do before the holidays so instead of doing rotations on Wednesday, I worked at the beauty salon. Mom took the news better than I expected. However, I promised to try to visit at Christmas.

Tim did come to the rescue though. He invited me over Thursday for dinner. I told him I had to be at the hospital from 5 p.m. to 5 a.m. but he said his family was used to working around a firefighter's schedule. They would love to have me over at 2 p.m., he said so I did not celebrate the holiday alone.

Tim's family took me in like a member of the family; they were so genuinely kind. His mother, Darlene, said it was about time they had the opportunity to meet the mystery woman that Tim was sneaking around with at Denny's most evenings. Tim blushed when he heard her

words. Darlene was short and round with brown curly hair that framed her face and it turned out that she was a fantastic cook. Her kitchen was large and even included a gas grill to cook burgers inside. His father, John, was tall and blond with sparkling green eyes. It was easy to see that Tim had inherited his father's handsome features.

Their home could not be cuter with a shelf in the living room that displayed different kinds of model fire trucks, from old-fashioned ones to modern vehicles. Family pictures hung along the hallway with one of John as a child wearing his father's fire hat, which of course, was way too big for his small head. Tim had a brother, Erik, who was 17 and a senior in high school. Both boys resembled each other and he also planned to be a firefighter when he graduated, just like his father and grandfather.

Over conversation, I learned that Tim had another brother who died in a motor vehicle accident three years before at the age of 16. Tim picked up a family photo - the last one taken while his brother was alive. He slowly shuffled over and sat on the couch next to me.

"This is Steven," he said in a weary voice.

His eyes never left the picture and I witnessed the love he still had for his brother.

"He was driving home from a football game the night he was killed," he explained. "Out of nowhere, a drunk driver hit him straight on the driver's side. His car rolled over, leaving him pinned inside and bleeding profusely from his neck."

I could sense the deep pain his face conveyed. This was a part of him that I had never seen - so vulnerable. I

scooted a little closer and took his free hand. I held it between both of my hands in my lap and remained quiet while he talked. I guess you could say my motherly instinct clicked in. I just wanted to ease his heartbreak.

"It wasn't fair," Tim said sucking in a breath. "He was only sixteen," he noted as his body slumped. "The other driver was so drunk that he didn't even know what he had done and emergency services was not called until someone else drove down the road.

By the time the call was made, it was too late," he whispered.

Tim's eyes peered into mine and he seemed embarrassed to have told me something so personal. I leaned over and gave him a hug. Then his arms circled my shoulders and he hugged me back. We stayed that way for some time and I thought I heard him cry. When his mother entered the living room to tell us dinner was ready, she noticed the picture on Tim's lap and sighed. She leaned down to give both of us a hug.

"It's time to eat," she said softly as she lifted the picture gently and placed it back where it belonged.

"Sorry," Tim whispered as his arms left my shoulders.

He did not look up and wiped his face. Then he stood and took my hands to help me up. He escorted me to the dining room where everyone sat down for supper. I found it astonishing that Tim did not really know me but was willing to share this information about his brother as well as his grief and I felt something tug at my heart.

At the dinner table, Darlene asked us to take each other's hands so she could say a prayer before we ate. I

peeked at Tim while the prayer was said and could see the gloom still on his face. Darlene looked up and noticed it too.

"Annette," Darlene said, "has my son ever told you how he got the chip on his front tooth?"

"Mom, not now," Tim said, his eyes flashing up at her.

His dad and brother began to laugh as his mom related the history of his youth.

"He was a rambunctious child growing up," she began as Tim wiggled uncomfortably in his seat. "He could never sit still and I constantly got phone calls from his school telling me how he teased the other kids."

"I wasn't that bad," Tim interrupted.

His mother shot a glance at her son as if to say, whatever.

"Well, this one day he was running down the halls with a couple of other boys. They were having a race to see who could get to the water fountain first."

Tim's face began to redden.

"His friend, Josh, got to the fountain first but Tim was a close second. He pushed Josh out of the way and grasped the knob while lowering his mouth to get a drink."

The laughter around the table grew louder.

"Josh tumbled away from the drinking fountain but was quick and when he noticed Tim take a drink, he ran back and slammed his head with his hand causing it to go down onto the sink."

"That wasn't funny," said Tim with an embarrassed smile. "You have no idea the pain I went through."

"I don't think Josh meant to hurt him," his mother continued. "Boys will be boys but the two of them were punished that day at school. Anyway, that's how his tooth got chipped and he's had that cute smile ever since."

"Can we eat now," begged Tim trying to change the subject.

"Fine," said his mom picking up a bowl of mashed potatoes. "We won't pick on you anymore… for a while."

I liked his family and the way his mom turned Tim's mood around. The rest of the meal was wonderful with good conversation and great food.

That night at the hospital, I took vitals for the nurses. They were celebrating the holiday with a table full of homemade food in the break room that each of the employees made and brought in from home. It was busy in the emergency room but not so much that we could not find time to sneak away and have a bite to eat. This was a different kind of Thanksgiving for me. I missed my parents and the sumptuous meals they prepared but I also enjoyed getting to know Tim's family and making friends with the hospital staff.

That morning when I got off work, I debated over whether I should call Aaron's father. Perhaps he could offer a plausible reason why his son had not written. Calling information, I found that Tom's number was unlisted. I was exhausted from working all night but my mind worked overtime. I could drive to Shawnee to talk to Tom but it would take an hour to get there one way and I did not have an extra two hours to spare. Maybe I was just being childish and should not get his father

involved but I really needed to know if Aaron was all right.

As I paced in circles around my room, I came to the conclusion that Aaron was a grown man, and his thoughtless action made me feel angry and hurt. With hands clutched firmly at my sides, I paced faster as if trying to wear down the carpet. I felt so betrayed. His silence was crushing my heart and my love. Then a rush of tears escaped my eyes. I had hoped and prayed for so long that he would just show up in my room one day and fall into my arms. I longed to hear from him and missed him terribly but realized that if I really wanted to stop hurting, I had to stop writing. My mind and body weary, I dropped into bed and quickly fell asleep.

Chapter 22
Home For The Holidays

I sat at Denny's and watched the pure white snow float like soft feathers to the ground. Christmas was just around the corner and the warmth of the restaurant was welcoming. A Christmas tree decorated with lights, and green and red paper chains stood inside the front door and little Italian lights hung around the ceiling blinking on and off. Along with a hint of piped-in Christmas music in the background, the restaurant reflected the holiday atmosphere.

Even though December's festivities were underway, it meant little to me as a paramedic student. Although I had a couple of weeks off school, clinical and ride-along time was still scheduled and of course, I still had my job at the beauty salon. Christmas was a busy time at the salon with many people requesting last minute perms and colors for the holidays. At school, I was studying geriatrics and how different older folks' bodies operated, as well as how to treat children, and handle labor and delivery. It was a lot to take in.

I sauntered to my booth where two Cokes already sat on the table. Removing my coat, I pushed it along the bench under the window before opening one of my books. The restaurant seemed peaceful that night with only a few booths filled. A couple sat at one booth staring into each other's eyes and a group of women who might have taken the evening off from their kids chatted quietly at another.

"Hey," said a familiar voice as he slipped off his jacket.

"Hey stranger."

I ordered a hamburger cut it in half and some fries assuming that Tim would help me eat them. He had a strange eating habit. I watched him pour mustard on his plate and dip his fries into it. I guess you would call this comfort food. It was not that we were all that hungry but it seemed easier to study while putting food in our mouths. We usually took turns ordering and sharing food whenever we met to study. It seemed like the logical thing to do.

We took out our books and answered the questions in the back of the chapter. I took my time looking up the answers but whenever I had trouble, Tim helped me out of the jam offering the answer.

"Okay, Annette explain how the respiratory system changes with an elderly person," Tim said leaning over the table and taking my book away from me. "You will be tested on this and you need to be able to answer without looking at your book."

I fought to keep it but he was too quick.

"Fine," I said giving up. "With aging, the chest wall becomes increasingly still as the bony thorax becomes more rigid and lung elastic recoil decreases." I was proud of myself, put my index finger in the air, licked it and said, "One for me!"

"Go on," he demanded. "You aren't finished yet." His eyes danced with delight waiting for my response.

"Um," I replied shrugging my shoulders with a blank look on my face. What could he be looking for? I

wondered searching my mind. I worried so much about passing the tests. Even though I was tired, I was grateful that Tim offered to help. I rubbed my temples in frustration.

"Annette, think of it this way," he said while I looked at him solemnly.

"Heart, kidneys, bones and musculoskeletal system. Think of your body and how it's going to age. Your heart function and kidneys will decline. Um, think of your grandma if you still have one alive and how she shrinks because of calcification to muscles and ligaments causing osteoporosis. Think of it this way: TMB."

He strummed his fingers on the tabletop anticipating my question.

"What?" I asked confused.

"TMB, silly," he laughed and then told me the meaning. "Too many birthdays!"

"What about this?" I added. "An instructor once told me that a heart only has a certain amount of beats just like a horse has only a certain number of jumps."

"I like that," he said smiling. "Can I use it?"

"Of course!"

Tim had a way of making me smile and that helped me to learn. Because learning from him was fun, I eagerly anticipated our study times - not only to learn but also for his company. For a couple of hours we reviewed labor and delivery procedures, and how to take care of a newborn baby.

Although we talked about school subjects, I sometimes caught him staring at me. When I'd glanced up at him,

he shyly lowered his eyes to peer at his book again. With our studying complete for the night, Tim helped me put on my coat and took my hand as we left our table. His hand felt warm and welcoming so I did not resist. He walked me to my car and then stopped letting his eyes explore my face.

"Be careful driving home tonight," he said.

He lowered his face toward mine and kissed me on the cheek. I'm sure my face turned pink with embarrassment. This was the first time he crossed the line toward being more personal.

"Thanks," I said getting into my car and closing the door. Then rolling down my window I yelled, "You be careful going home too."

I noticed his face draw up into a big smile showing his chipped tooth.

I manage to get a few days off work over Christmas so I visited my folks for a couple days. Although putting away the books was difficult, I missed them so much and was elated to see them. The house was beautifully decorated in green and red. Of course, they had a real Christmas tree. My mom said she would never have a fake tree in her home while she was alive. Her favorite was the Colorado blue spruce and she decorated it with big old-fashioned tree lights instead of the little Italian ones that seemed so popular.

When I was young, we made sequined ornaments and that was what mostly lined the tree. We also glued glitter on pinecones and hung them from the limbs and to top off the tree, mom added colorful red bows.

We always attended church on Christmas Eve and opened one gift each – usually pajamas - from under the tree. After we put them on, we watched *It's a Wonderful Life*.

Dad always fell asleep in the middle of the movie but mom and I nestled on the couch, sharing a blanket and enjoying the story. This time, mom made dad wake up and go to bed as we sat huddled together. As always, we kept Kleenex nearby to wipe the tears we shared. When the movie ended, mom put her hand on my lap, covered my hands and smiled.

"It's so good to have you home, sweetie," she said.

I watched her grab a Kleenex to wipe tears from her face.

"I'm still crying from the movie," she said hiding her true emotions.

I knew they were happy tears because I was home but I did not want to ruin the moment for her. Mom was sentimental like that.

"I love being back," I said reaching over to plant a kiss on her cheek. "I've really missed you too."

"So how have you been?" she asked.

I moved my legs around to change position on the couch.

"Busy, mom," I replied readjusting the blanket. "School is a lot harder than I expected but I love it." I did not realize what expression showed on my face.

"I can tell," she said smiling. "You're glowing. Your eyes tell me how much you enjoy what you're learning. And what about your love life?" she asked unexpectedly.

"I don't mean to pry but you haven't talked about Aaron lately."

The smile suddenly dropped from my face and mom took my hand.

"What's wrong with me, mom?" I asked, hot tears filling my eyes. "I haven't heard from him in over five months."

Mom scooted over, wrapped her arms around me and let my head fall to her shoulder.

"I know sweetie. Love is so hard to understand," she said as I began to sob loudly. "But you're young and will love again," she assured rocking me back and forth.

Why would I ever want to love again? I wondered. Didn't she realize that I never wanted to hurt like this again?

"Why hasn't he called me?"

"Oh, honey," she soothed pulling me closer. "I'm so sorry you're hurting like this." Mom held me quietly for a few moments.

"There is nothing wrong with a good cry, Annette. I believe it cleanses the soul."

Finally, she pushed me gently back and looked into my eyes. She handed me a Kleenex and moved some hair from my face tucking it behind my ear.

"I think you should put your energy into your studies right now," she advised. "Maybe this is a good thing. Otherwise, your mind would be on Aaron instead of school."

I looked at her questioningly.

"After all, you keep telling me how hard your studies have been. I don't think I could ever remember all that you're learning right now… and I am so proud of you."

"Thanks, mom," I said putting on a half smile.

I knew she was right. I did not tell her that I finally decided to stop writing to Aaron, although I did send him a Christmas card. I did not write much, except to say that I hoped he was having a great holiday and that I was still praying for him. I had no expectations about hearing from him again.

Chapter 23
Life Without Aaron

January 1997 - Happy New Year. At school, we learned practical exercises pretending a patient was critically bleeding and using the techniques we learned to stop it, including raising the extremities, applying direct pressure and then putting on a pressure dressing… and we could not forget the oxygen. One of the students played the patient and a couple of others pretended to be on scene learning hands-on how to stop the bleeding.

In another scenario, a patient stopped breathing and we had to go through the proper procedure: the head-tilt/chin lift or the jaw-thrust maneuver, as well as inserting a nasal or oral airway before bagging and intubation, the latter meaning the placement of a flexible plastic tube into the windpipe to maintain an open airway. Of course, we did not attempt to put a nasal or oral airway into each other! For that, we used a mannequin.

I was so busy that my days and nights soon became mixed up. I had no idea what time it was most of the time or even what day of the week it might be. During my pediatrics rotation in the children's ward, I found this the most difficult of all the clinicals. I walked around with nurses to take vitals and check up on the young patients. I was surprised to see so many sick children. They were all ages and most of them had a parent or guardian sitting with them. The parents were so kind when I entered their rooms and let me practice taking vitals on their children. Most of the kids were lovable and

happy. A few were hurting too badly to even care that I was there.

One of them bothered me more than the rest. Only six months old, this baby lay in a crib with wires and tubes in any and every crevice of his body. Picture a child laying in a bed with IV's, ECG leads and other lines running from his or her body and hearing the constant beeping of machines. That was his world. He was born handicapped and could not breathe on his own. There was a hole in his throat with a tube inserted that was attached to a ventilator that breathed for him.

I watched as the nurse took his vitals and checked all of his tubing. He jerked suddenly and the motion lasted for at least two minutes. The nurse explained that he often had seizures. I did not see his parents so I asked about them. This poor child was the youngest of four children. Because his mom was so busy, she visited whenever she could. I drew near to his crib and stroked his arm. He lay motionless, except for his chest moving up and down from the oxygen being introduced into his lungs.

"Can I pick him up?" I asked fighting back tears. The baby lay so still when he was not having a seizure.

"No dear," the nurse replied as she took his temperature. "Come on. We have a few more patients to take care of now."

I followed her from room to room but that child was still on my mind and I could not find peace while on that floor. I was anxious for that shift to end.

"What would I do if I had to help a child like that when I was working?" I wondered.

It was a painful thought but I had to push it aside so I could continue my rounds. I felt so mentally tired by the end of the day that I just wanted to go home and fall into bed. When my shift was over, I gladly said goodbye anxious to get out of there.

By the time February arrived, I thought I must be delirious because I often forgot what day it was. Tim just laughed and reminded me that we were more than half way through the course.

"Soon all of this will only be a memory," he said.

In the meantime my life would not change, only consisting of work, school, studying and clinical. That month, I was allowed to spend time on the labor and delivery floor. It was amazing to see all of the equipment it took to help someone have a baby but I had no idea how my adrenalin would react when I watched a birth for the first time. The hospital staff placed a monitor on the mother-to-be that registered the baby's heartbeat and another that let them know if the baby was in stress. An IV was inserted into her arm and an ECG monitor was hooked up as well.

The expectant woman told the nurse that she felt like pushing. The doctor had not arrived yet so the nurse told her to keep her legs together to decrease the urge. I helped the nurse place a sterile sheet under her and lifted her legs into the stirrups. The bed had a moving part that folded down turning it into a deliver bed. I helped prep her and finally the doctor appeared wearing a pair of

blue plaid shorts and a matching polo shirt with mesh ventilation on the back. I guessed that he was out playing golf when he got the call and rushed over without changing. The expectant mother relaxed when she spotted him.

Slipping on a pair of gloves, the doctor asked her slid down toward the end of the bed with her legs in the stirrups. Then he used his fingers to determine how much she had dilated.

"Yep, you're dilated to a ten," he said smiling, "and I can feel a head so whenever you experience the next pain, go ahead and push."

The woman nodded and within seconds she cried out. Her body tightened and she pushed like she was trying to have a bowel movement.

"One more time," coaxed the doctor. "I can see the head."

I had to peek and sure enough, I saw black hair trying to push its way out of her. I could not believe my eyes. She tensed her body again and the doctor put his hands under the slippery head that was being pushed out. He turned it a little and I noticed a shoulder slip through. Then the other shoulder appeared followed by the rest of the body that shot out like a slippery football. The doctor let his hands roll with the movement and skillfully caught the newborn infant.

Next was the cord, just like we learned in school. The nurse took two clips and set them in place before cutting the cord with a knife. The baby cried and the mother held out her arms, anxious to hold him. My adrenalin

pumped so hard watching this birth that I thought I might never sleep that night. Later, I shared this experience with Tim and he told me of a similar birth that occurred once with his dad on the fire truck. He gave me a hug and I had to admit, it felt good.

By the time March rolled around, I realized that I only had a couple of months of school left and I had to admit that Aaron was far from my mind. I was told the National Registry test was a real bear to pass. Along with ambulance rides and clinicals, I was finally allowed to conduct rotations with the doctors in the operating room. What an experience getting up so early in the morning, arriving at the hospital, and putting on those blue paper-like pants and shirts with matching hats and booties to ensure I was sterile.

I waited in a corner of the operating room watching the technicians as they took out tables and placed sterile equipment on them. They covered them up while waiting for the doctor. Next they brought in and prepped the patient. The technicians ensured that the IV line was in place and working properly.

I stood next to the anesthesiologist while he showed me his intubation technique and then watched as I put the tube into the patient's trachea for him. It was imperative to learn this technique and the best way was with a doctor who did it all the time. While learning the procedure in school, I missed a couple of times. In the operating room, the doctor made it clear that I only had one chance to get it right. If I missed, he would intubate the patient himself and I could try again on his next one.

What a difference doing this on a real person verses a manikin. I had four patients that morning and was successful with two of them. Thank heavens I still had a few more rotations, so I could practice and learn more.

The neat thing about being in the operating room was that after the intubation, I could stay to see the operation preformed. I watched a knee replacement, which was pretty exciting. The doctors actually burned the skin over the knee through the muscle and slid the skin down on both sides to expose the bone. The only thing I did not like was the far from pleasant smell of burning flesh and muscle.

With all the clinical work and the need to take more time off work, I was thankful that my customers at the beauty salon continued to show patience. A couple of them occasionally let other beauticians do their hair if they had plans and could not change their appointments but they always promise that I could take over again the following week. I was learning so much at the hospital and on the ambulance that I soon became a storyteller relating some of my adventures to my patrons. They seemed most interested and always asked to hear what I learned each week.

By April I still had my clinicals and rotations to finish, which would probably take a few more months. At school, I practiced practical skills for the upcoming test. The students were given a sheet of paper that showed what they needed to do and how many points they would lose if they missed something important. We would be tested on things like patient assessment for medical and trauma. We needed to prove that we could properly

ventilate a patient, show we could work a cardiac monitor and knew what to do with different rhythms. Our IV skills and measuring proper doses of medication would be examined along with how to control spinal immobilization and bleeding control with shock. Even though I practiced the techniques many times, I sometimes felt that I forgot something perhaps due to nervousness or lack of sleep. I just plain worried that I would not pass after everything I'd learned and experienced.

Some days, I managed to find time to study at the firehouse with Tim's father acting as our instructor. I enjoyed this because he let us practice on some of the firefighters as patients. It helped to hear the technique these guys used to remember what to do when they were first learning. We also spent more time at Denny's quizzing each other with tests that we build for each other. Soon I forgot what my bed looked like and thought of Denny's as my home.

The past year had been a formidable one. My days were so hectic that sometimes I could not remember if I stopped to eat. I was so physically, mentally and emotionally spent that when I tried to sleep, my mind refused to rest as it rehashed everything I learned. I forgot what it was like to relax and watch a good movie or even talk on the phone. I knew that if I could not handle the strain, I risked failing the final test.

Over time, I realized that my life was complete and fulfilling without Aaron. On my calendar, Tim's name appeared often for study dates, which always made me smile.

We had fallen into a comfortable routine. Whether picking me up for school or meeting him there, we laughed a lot and started to finish each other's sentences as if we had been together for years. Holding hands and sharing a light kiss goodbye had become comfortable. Tim seemed devoted to me with the promise that I would pass the course, which helped me feel more secure about my future. Life might have been difficult with the stress of school but our relationship grew without us even realizing it.

Chapter 24
More Than Friends?

Finally, May arrived and with it, my last month of classes. I could finally see the light at the end of the tunnel and my initial exuberance returned. I would not take the National Registry test until August but I still had to study and finish my practicals. Meanwhile, the teacher prepared us with our written exams. The hardest part would be questions with four possible answers, with two of them sounding right but only one that was correct. Yuck. Why do they have to make it so difficult? I thought.

My ambulance ride-alongs were with some amiable medics. They let me insert the IV's and in one case, allowed me to give aspirin and nitro to the first chest patient I ever had. One call involved a full arrest and my paramedic teachers decided I should be in charge. An old gentleman was found lying on a bed. I did not see his chest rising so I put my hand by his face but could not feel him breathing. I then felt for a pulse on his neck but there was none. I ordered the firefighters to place him on the floor and began CPR.

With the others working around me, I felt a little overwhelmed trying to remember everything I learned. One of firefighters took out a bag valve mask, attached it to oxygen and started bagging the patient as another did chest compressions. At the same time, I got out my intubation equipment and my first attempt was successful. I requested that an IV be put in as I intubated

the patient. Another firefighter took out ECG leads and pads so we could determine the man's cardiac rhythm.

The compressions were halted momentarily, so we could visualize what the rhythm was. It showed as pulse less V-tach (a fast and life-threatening heartbeat) so I administered shock.

The firefighter that bagged the patient with oxygen took over with that again. We stopped to check the ECG monitor, which still read V-tach so I ordered CPR for a couple of minutes before I shocked him again. When we looked again, the monitor went to asystole, which meant there was no heart rhythm. I again ordered CPR and injected epinephrine - a hormone and neurotransmitter to stimulate his heart - into his IV. Thankfully, the monitor began to show a pulse. I stopped the CPR and felt for it. It was weak but there was one.

We quickly placed the patient on a gurney with monitor, pulse oximeter (that indirectly monitored the oxygen saturation of the patient's blood) and oxygen in hand. He still could not breathe on his own so one of the firefighters continued to use the bag valve mask to force oxygen into his lungs. While still monitoring the patient and taking vitals, we drove with lights and sirens blaring to the hospital. Four people were crammed in the back of the ambulance that day doing everything they could to keep the man alive. What a rush!

I had quite the story to share with my roommates when I finally arrived home and could not wait to call my mother as well. The next day at school, I ran into Tim's

arms and told him of my experience too. He responded by saying I could be his partner anytime. Then he kissed me - a kiss that was much different and definitely more passionate than any we shared before.

By the time June arrived, I could practically do what was expected of me in my sleep. However, I did not want to be over confident. At the same time, I felt worn out. Glancing in the mirror, I noticed lines under my eyes. Even so, my fervor grew with the knowledge that I had taken in everything I learned.

At the end of the month, I took the final test. Only ten people out of the fifteen in the class graduated and thankfully, I was one of them. My parents attended the ceremony and were so happy for me. Afterward, they took me out for dinner and I introduced them to Tim.

The year had flown by like whirlwind and the only thing left was the National Registry test in August, which was known as the most difficult to pass. I had to keep studying to ensure that I did not forget anything.

The following Monday morning, I lingered in bed while my roommates took off for school. Sleeping in and waking up slowly was deeply appreciated. The morning seemed peaceful with no one around as I dragged my slippers into the kitchen to make some coffee. I looked forward to a long hot bath and perhaps relaxing with a good book. The phone rang and I smiled knowing mom would be on the other end. I missed my Monday talks with her.

"Hey mom," I said as I headed for a chair by kitchen table.

"Who?" a male voice responded.

"Umm, good morning," I giggled before taking a swig of coffee. My heart actually jumped for joy at the sound of his voice.

"Good morning," Tim replied. "I haven't seen you in a couple of days now that school is out and I missed talking to you. So how are you?"

As soon as he said that, memories of the last year resurfaced in my mind. I saw him sitting across the table at Denny's testing me and helping me understand things that I thought I would never get. I really appreciated Tim and all he put up with from me to help me pass.

"I'm good," I said playing with the phone cord.

"Are you nervous about the test next month?"

"To tell you the truth, I am," I admitted. "You?"

"Hell no, I got it all together. Remember, my dad is a firefighter."

"I wish I had your confidence."

"I could come over and help you study… we could especially go over the practical things like mouth-to-mouth resuscitation," he said laughing.

I chose to ignore that comment and simply asked: "What's up?"

"Just wondered if you made any plans for today?"

"Yeah, I did," I noted and heard him sigh on the other end. "I thought I would relax, take a nice hot bath and do nothing. That's my big plan."

"How about going for some lunch then? I know of a good Chinese food restaurant."

I detected the longing to his voice.

"Not Denny's?" I teased.

"Ugh."

"Sure," I said with enthusiasm.

"Cool. See you in a couple of hours."

I quickly took a shower, instead of the long awaited bath, and put on some nice smelling dusting powder and perfume. Donning my blue jeans, I looked for a blouse to make me look pretty. I had grown tired of always wearing my uniform shirt when I saw him. After hearing his voice on the phone, I realized that I missed him and could not wait to see his familiar smile.

At noon I heard a knock at the front door and when I opened it, there was Tim smiling with his chipped tooth showing.

"Ready?" he asked as he took my hand to escort me outside.

Wearing blue jeans and his favorite red jersey, he quickly pecked me on the lips and led me to his car. As we drove to the restaurant, he was so animated that he seemed like a little boy who just caught his first fish. When we pulled into the parking lot, he told me not to get out and ran around the car to get my door for me. At the entrance of the establishment, a happy Buddha statue greeted us. After being escorted to our seats, I noticed a display of aesthetic Chinese ornaments and the soothing pastel walls. Just smelling the food in the warmers made my mouth water. It was an all-you-can-eat restaurant so I got in line, filled my plate and returned to the booth. I took the fork out of the rolled up napkin and dug in.

"Annette, you can't use a fork when eating Chinese food," Tim said taking it from my hand. "It's not American."

He grabbed a pair of chopsticks and handed them to me. I tried to hold the food between the two sticks in my clumsy hands but by the time they reached my mouth, the food fell back onto the plate. I could not help giggling.

"Like this," Tim instructed. He picked up little bites of food and actually got them into his mouth. I watched and tried to follow his lead. It was fun, even if I could not hold them correctly but I finally got the hang of it. As we ate, we talked about the upcoming test and how quickly the past year had gone by. The desert table was full of cakes, pudding, fruits and ice cream. I tried some bananas in strawberry jelly and my taste buds exploded. Then the waitress came over and passed us each a fortune cookie along with the bill. Tim opened his cookie and read his fortune aloud.

"Good fortune will come your way," he laughed showing me the piece of paper. "If I pass and finally become a paramedic, then I can concur with this fortune." He picked up my cookie and placed it in my hand.

"Come on, your turn. Let's have fun with this."

Removing the cellophane, I cracked open my cookie. I read it to myself and felt his stare.

"No, Annette. If you want your fortune to come true, you have to read it out loud."

I rolled my eyes and cleared my throat.

"Good things come to those who work hard," I said tilting my head and giving him a strange stare. "Of course, if you work hard for something the outcome would be good," I added sarcastically. "What kind of fortune is that?"

"It's just for entertainment, Annette. Where is your sense of humor?"

When we finished, Tim took me to the firehouse. There was a park behind it and a softball game was in session. It seemed that the firefighters enjoyed playing against each other when they were not working. I stood with Tim's father cheering on the team as Tim played. When the game ended, we decided to take the walking trail that encircled the park. We walked close but not touching while Tim told me more about how he came from a long line of firefighters. I explained how the Oklahoma bombing sparked my interested in becoming a paramedic. Then we shared our feelings on the day the bombing occurred.

"My dad's truck was one of the first on scene," said Tim. "The firefighters had practiced drills for something like that but never in their wildest dreams did they expect to actually experience that kind of devastation first hand." Wiping blond hair from his eyes he added, "At least not a bombing like the one right here in Oklahoma City."

"I saw on the news how bad it was," I noted. "That's when I drove to the city to see if I could be of some assistance."

"My dad said they helped survivors get out of the building and triaged people to see who needed to go to

the hospitals first," Tim continued. "They had so many casualties; it was hard to get enough ambulances to take them."

"Well, I was upset that they wouldn't let me help," I said, the anger I felt that day surging up again as I spoke of it. "At the very least, I could have taken someone to the hospital. I told them I wanted to help but they pushed me away."

"Sorry to hear that," he said. "I bet they could have used you. I mean I know they needed more ambulances. Why couldn't they be more inventive?"

"Exactly," I responded shrugging my shoulders in agreement. "On TV, I saw firefighters carrying hurt children and adults that were bleeding. I really wanted to help."

I noticed him wince before he went on.

"Did you know that some of the survivors had to have limbs amputated on site without anesthetic so they could be freed from the rubble?"

I felt the back of my throat go dry and tears formed in the back of my eyes.

"No," I whispered. We walk in silence for a few moments before he continued.

"My dad said that after they found the easy survivors, they climbed around the wreckage looking and yelling for anyone who might be trapped under it. They actually heard some voices yell back," he said and his face lightened up. "They were excited and hoped to rescue them. Some of the firefighters actually touched a few survivors' hands through the floor. They began moving the wreckage around them but it was a lot harder and

took much longer than they anticipated. Then there was another bomb scare and they were told to evacuate immediately. Some of the guys initially refused but the police made them leave."

I heard Tim catch his breath before he went on in a lower and slower tone.

"They left with the promise to come back and rescue those people but it took too long and some of them died."

His face reflected their pain and knew it was this kind of sensitivity about him that I loved. We walked most of the way around the field and saw a few kids on swings at the playground in the park. A couple of people offered a hello as they ran past us.

"Have you ever had a girlfriend?" I asked catching him off guard. I really felt the need to change the subject. Tim turned toward me and smiled.

"Yeah… but we broke up a long while ago."

"What happened?" I asked with genuine interest.

"I don't really know. I guess we just wanted different things. She definitely didn't like the idea of me being a firefighter and I really tried to escape my destiny. We were both in college and I think she hoped I would get a degree in anything but that. I did take business courses and tried to please her but hey, it's in my blood," he said smiling. "What about you?"

"Yeah, his name is Aaron." I replied sucking in a deep breath. "Actually, he's in the army and in Afghanistan right now. We were writing but I haven't heard from him since August." My body tensed and Tim did not respond. Then I told him all about Aaron. He listened and when I

cried, he held me to console me. I felt a peacefulness settle over me as I spilled my guts to him.

"Do you know what I was thinking?" he said after wiping tears from my face.

"No," I sniffed.

He put his arm around my waist and we resumed walking.

"I was thinking of the first day of class and when I met you. You wouldn't give me the time of day, just offering little answers that I couldn't respond to."

"I'm glad you didn't give up on me," I whispered slipping my arm around him and giving a gentle squeeze.

"I remember everything about the first couple of months of school and seeing how beautiful you looked. I wanted to get to know you better but you were on a mission of some kind and wouldn't let anyone get close."

I nodded with a shaky grin. The memory of those first months of school and how I longed for letters from Aaron ran through my mind.

"I then took it upon myself to go to Denny's but you were not very receptive.

Remember?"

"I'm sorry, Tim" I responded. I looked up at him and could feel my face flush.

"You don't understand," he said moving a piece of hair from my face and placing it behind my ear. "That was the beginning of a beautiful relationship. I told myself to be patient and when I thought about it, I knew you were right. It was important to keep our minds on studying. That was definitely not the time to try for a girlfriend."

"I know for me, there was no way I could think about a relationship while trying to study. I had no idea how much of my life would be taken over when I signed up for school."

We both laughed aloud.

"The rumors were correct, weren't they?" he mused. "We had no life during paramedic training but we really got to know each other on a friendship level. Now I hope to know you on other levels."

Tim was right. We were able to learn about each other without the awkwardness of being an item. We could finish each other's sentences, and knew each other's favorite foods and colors. We quizzed each other, not worrying if we hurt each other's feelings, only with the anticipation of passing our course and in the process, we realized that we also had the same interests.

"Hey Romeo, we still have to study you know," I said lightheartedly recalling the test still ahead of us. "We aren't out of the woods yet."

Tim smiled, stopped and drew me close. He gave me a passionate kiss and I had to catch my breath. When finished, he took my hand in his.

"I can wait," he said as we continued on the trail.

The rest of the month, we studied together and practiced some of the practical exams, pointing out any errors we made or what we forgot to say so we would pass. We took long walks holding hands and talked about our desires for the future, which seemed to be the same. We both wanted a job helping people. Although I did not want to be a firefighter, we both aspired to be

paramedics. His inspiration stemmed from belonging to a long line of firefighters. Mine was due to the tragedy that occurred in our state. There we were - two young people trying to find our way in the world.

We kept our focus on our goal but little by little, I realized we were becoming much more than friends.

Chapter 25
A New Love Grows

At the beauty salon, the girls held a graduation party for me, even though I still needed to pass the National Registry exam. It seemed they had faith that I could do it. Even some of my customers attended to celebrate my victory. Judy agreed to let me work part time around my rotating hours when I finally landed a job as well as pencil in customers when my name was on the books for that day. But that meant my regular Friday and Saturday customers who wanted shampoos and sets would need to find someone else. Fortunately, Veronica and Betty were more than happy to fill in. I told Judy that I could start with one day a week until I grew accustomed to my new schedule working twenty-four hours at a shot and she agreed.

Finally August 26 arrived – time to take the big test. Tim picked me up so we could take the written exam in the morning and the practical exam in the afternoon.

"You okay?" he asked as we drove to the examination site.

"Nervous," I said fidgeting in my seat. My heart pounded, my hands were sweaty and anxiety seized me. Glancing at my wristwatch the time read 8:30 a.m. and the test starts at 9 a.m. There were dark clouds above us emitting a few scattered raindrops. Could they be a sign of a bad day, I wondered?

"You're going to do just fine," Tim said patting my knee and smiling. "Anything you want to go over?"

The one thing I liked about Tim was how he always kept my confidence up.

"No," I said taking in a deep breath. "I'm just afraid I've been studying so much and going over the material in my head so many times that I might get all this information mixed up."

We drove into the parking lot and quickly ran inside the building between the sprinkles. Tim took my hand as we made our way to the testing room. The large room was filled with desks and all kinds of people: young ones like me, older folks, men and women, who came from different schools. Tim kissed me quickly and then we sat down next to each other.

"Think positive," he whispered before the doors shut.

An instructor told us what was expected of us before the test began. We had to move around so there were a few empty desks between us. With only a couple of pencils on our desks and everything else on the floor, it was time to get started. The test included one hundred and fifty questions and we were only allotted two and a half hours to finish it. I glanced up at Tim and gave him a grave smile. We could only face forward or down at our tests so I quickly readjusted in my seat.

The answer paper was passed around first and then the test. One instructor sat at the front of the room and another in the back so no one would think of cheating. Nervously, I read the questions and filled in the circles to the correct answers. Sometimes I needed to read a question several times to understand what answer was required. And just as I'd heard, two answers were

basically correct. I just had to choose the one that was totally correct.

Before long, I was surprised to see someone walk to the front of the classroom and place his test face down on the desk.

"Are you sure you don't want to check this over one more time?" asked the instructor glancing at the clock on the wall. "You still have an hour and a half to finish."

The guy shook his head no and walked out of the room. Thirty minutes later, another person did the same, while I was only half way through with an hour to go. My mind kept reading and re-reading, trying not to make more out of the questions than necessary as I answered them. Sometimes the words seemed blurry to me. Thirty minutes remained and slowly more students left their seats. I even noticed Tim walk to the front of the room and my anxiety returned. My body felt warm, my hands were sweaty and I wiped them on my pants. I glanced one last time at my answers and noticed that only ten minutes were left. I knew I had no time to re-read it so I brought up my paper. Tim was outside waiting for me.

"You all right?" he asked putting his arms around me and offering a much-needed hug.

I slumped my head on his shoulder and sighed loudly. "Yeah, I guess so."

"Are you hungry?" he coaxed letting me go and taking my hand to follow him to the car. We drove to McDonald's knowing we only had an hour before we had to take our practical tests. Quickly, we stood in line, got our food and grabbed a seat.

"I'm a nervous wreck," I said as I ate my chicken salad.

"You could have fooled me," he replied with a wink. "You looked beautiful. I couldn't tell you were nervous."

He took another bite of his burger and popped in a fry before he spoke again. I focused on him wishing I had his confidence.

"It's almost over, girlfriend. Soon you'll be able to call yourself a paramedic and live your dream."

We rushed back to the testing building for another grueling five hours. We had to wait behind closed doors for our turn to demonstrate the procedures and hoped we passed.

Afterward, I thought I might collapse. Tim suggested we do something to celebrate because the hard part was behind us. We went out for Chinese food and then to the movies. What a way to end a day - by eating, laughing and no studying!

I took off the next day of work, opting instead to relax with Tim. He told me to make sure I had my riding boots on. When he arrived, we drove to his grandmother's ranch.

Her name was Clair, a sweet white-haired woman and a romantic. Her hair was tied up in a bun and she wore blue jeans with a plaid shirt tucked into her pants along with cowboy boots. Clair had prepared a picnic basket for us with cheese, crackers, strawberries, grapes and a bottle of wine. She led us to the barn where she already had two saddled horses waiting. The barking of a dog,

neighing of the horses and a cat running past my legs re-enforced the ranch atmosphere.

"They're beautiful," I said petting the face of a black-haired horse. "What are their names?"

"Don't laugh," said Clair. "Sonny and Cher." She held onto Cher as I climbed into the saddle. Tim acted like a pro jumping into his saddle in no time.

"You know son," she noted turning toward him. "This is how your grandfather landed me. He took me riding and this is the same lunch he prepared for me," she added with a giggle. "The only thing is he didn't tell me he couldn't ride a horse. I, on the other hand, understood horses and knew how to ride them. So we trotted down the trail and he managed to keep up but once we reached the open field, I hit my horse with my heels and took off galloping. Your grandpa tried to do the same but eventually fell off his horse. I believed it was my fault and apologized."

She stopped for a moment, gathered her thoughts and gazed straight out in front of her toward the trail.

"We decided to stop and have lunch. He poured me some wine and said he wanted to make a toast but instead pulled a ring from his pocket, got down on his knees and proposed. How could I say no? He was so romantic and I figured I owed him for making him fall," she laughed.

Clair glanced quickly at me and winked before she wished us a good day. She yelled loudly and hit my horse on the behind to make her move. That was all it took and Tim's horse followed quickly behind mine. I hoped she wasn't hinting for Tim to follow in his grandfather's footsteps. As we rode out of sight, I noticed her waving.

We walked our horses along the trails and galloped through the open fields. As the wind blew through my hair, I was overtaken with the beauty of the countryside. Our conversation along the way was pleasant and filled with laughter. Finally, Tim found an appropriate place for us to stop and helped me off my horse. I felt a little intimidated by what his grandmother had said but tried to look unruffled.

"Tim?" I said as he took the food from the basket. "Did your grandfather really propose to your grandma that way?"

He smiled and handed me a plastic glass with a little wine in it.

"Yeah," he replied handing over a napkin with some cheese and grapes.

"Thank you… mm, I don't want to hurt your feelings or your grandma's but I'm not ready to get married yet."

"I'm sorry about that," Tim laughed playfully. "She's just a romantic, and wants to see me happy and married. She wants great grandbabies."

I could not help blushing

"Don't worry," he soothed trying to make me feel comfortable. "I don't have a ring on me."

It was the acceptance in his voice that made me feel so comfortable. We ate lunch while Tim talked about his grandparents and the farm. Afterward, he helped me onto my horse and we rode back to the barn. Then we walked the horses in the corral for a bit before we fed them. In the barn, Tim showed me how to separate the chunks of hay before throwing them into the troughs. As I did, he left to get a couple of buckets of oats for them to

eat. He looked so at home on the ranch. As we watched the horses eat, his grandmother entered the barn.

"It's so beautiful here," I said gazing out toward the meadow. "And thank you for letting us go riding."

"It is peaceful here," she agreed with a smile and nod. "You seldom see cars drive down this street. In fact, it's so quiet that you can think without interruption."

I kept my eyes on her as she walked to the shed. She took out a couple of shovels and my curiosity kicked in when she walked back to us.

"Now you two can help me clean up before dinner," she said handing a shovel to each of us.

"Clean up?" I asked, eyes wide.

"The manure," she said smiling. "Otherwise, the smell can get pretty harsh. Tim, you can show her how to do this since you've done it before."

Then she walked away only to return with a wheelbarrow. Tim lifted up a heap of manure and dumped it into the wheelbarrow. It must have been around 6 p.m. because the sun had dropped more than half way in the sky spreading long shadows on the ground below. We worked quietly while Clair brushed the horses.

"Thanks kids, for helping me," she said looking pleased before leaving to go to the house.

We finally finished the awful job and I leaned on my shovel to inspect Tim. Shadows covered half of his face but he still looked handsome. I enjoyed watching the boy in him for a change, instead of the man. Memories of him and school flooded my mind. I appreciated his help with

school and for being there when I was upset over Aaron. His face turned toward me and he caught me staring.

"Is everything all right?" he asked.

I could tell he wondered what I was thinking.

"Yeah, but I'm getting hungry."

"You're always hungry," he laughed, satisfied with my answer.

I shifted my weight from one foot to the other, a little embarrassed.

"Your grandma is wonderful."

"Yes she is," he nodded. "Come on. Let's see what she has to eat."

Tim took my hand and we made our way into the house. Inside, the scent of pot roast filled the kitchen. Clair's kitchen was decorated with colorful fruit and vegetable wallpaper on one wall and yellow paint on the others. An old milk can stood by the back door. When I asked her about it, she explained that it was the last one from the milk farm her father owned so it held fond memories of growing up. Although she did not enjoy getting up in the mornings to milk the cows, she said she did miss the fresh milk and eggs they gathered every day from their animals.

"Hope you two are hungry?" Clair said. "Go wash your hands for dinner."

She did not have to ask twice and in a matter of moments, we sat around the table. We enjoyed a wonderful meal, which was followed by hugs before we left for home. Tim seemed quiet on the way with the radio blaring to take up the silence. We both had a lot on our minds so this was understandable. Instead of taking

me home, we arrived at the firehouse. As we walked toward the building, Tim dragged his feet and I followed his pace. The dark sky was lit with a million stars and a big full moon. The only sounds were our footsteps and the crickets.

"Annette," he said stopping in his tracks under an outside light and turning to face me.

"You know you mean a lot to me, correct?" He took my hands in his and his eyes searched mine as if he was looking for my soul. I was not sure that I was prepared for what he might say. My heart was not ready for someone to hurt me again yet I seemed to be drawn to him.

"You mean a lot to me too."

Tim smiled, his hands leaving mine and cradling my cheeks. He sucked in a deep breath like he was taking in my scent before his lips touched mine. I leaned into his body and molded into his kiss. It was a long one and before I knew it, he kissed me again. Our arms wrapped around each other tightly. Then he backed up a little and his eyes focused on my face.

"I know I told you I wouldn't ask you to marry me yet but I didn't tell you I wouldn't fall in love with you."

Something inside my chest ached as if someone hit me. I recalled hearing these words from Aaron and looked away for a moment hoping to hide my pain.

"You don't have to say anything, Annette. I don't have any expectations. I just want you to know how I feel."

The weight of his words hung heavily in the air. I heard a hint of sadness in his voice and my heart hurt for him.

"Give me time," I asked with a faint smile. "I'm falling for you too but I'm just not sure I'm ready for love yet."

Tim smiled and took my hand back into his.

"That's all I needed to hear," he said a little more chipper.

We slowly walked back to the car and drove in silence to my home. Before I got out of the car, he leaned over and kissed me goodbye. Then I stood on the porch and watched him drive away. I spent the rest of the night alone in my room filled with images of the day and with confidence that he was there for me whenever I needed him. Tim seemed somehow drawn to me and had lit a flame that I valiantly tried not to catch. I knew he had stronger feelings for me than I did for him but somehow, he knew how to handle it. Even so, I realized deep down that I might be falling in love.

Chapter 26
New Beginnings

It took four weeks before I received my results from the National Registry. Too nervous to open the envelope, I met Tim at our favorite Chinese restaurant. We decided to open our envelopes first to make sure we had something to celebrate. My heart pounded yet Tim appeared unbelievably calm.

"Okay," I said waving the envelope in the air as we sat in his car.

He nodded fully enjoying my playfulness.

"When I count to three, we'll open them together," I said. I took a deep breath and then another. Then I opened my mouth to speak but nothing came out so I breathed in deeply a third time.

"Stop stalling," Tim teased.

"Okay, ready, set."

"No, you're supposed to count to three," he reminded me and zealously swatted the top of my head with his envelope.

I was so delighted to finally receive the results but was reluctant to see if I actually passed. The more I stalled, the longer it would be before I knew if I failed. Finally, Tim grabbed my hands.

"We will count together," he decided.

"One, two, three!" we yelled like children with my voice louder than his.

Quickly, we tore open our envelopes. My eyes scanned the paper missing most of what the letter said, checking just to see if I passed. I realized I missed a lot but I only wanted to see two words. When I did, my eyes filled with tears.

"I passed!" I screamed jumping in my seat. I grabbed the back of his head, pulled him toward me and kissed him hard.

"Me too!" he yelled back kissing me for a second time.

We hugged and bounced around in the car feeling the joy of the moment. I felt indebted to Tim for helping me to succeed and relished being able to share this triumphant achievement with him.

"I think this is just about the happiest day of my life!" I squealed.

"I am really happy for both of us," Tim replied.

"Can we go eat now?" I asked calming down somewhat from my revelry.

"Yep, we sure can."

With arms wrapped around each other we strolled into the restaurant for our celebration feast. After getting our drinks, we headed to the smorgasbord. We sat across from each other taking bites and sharing blissful glances.

"Do you have any idea where you want to work?" asked Tim.

"I think EMSA," I replied shaking my head.

That was the only private ambulance company in Oklahoma City. Otherwise, I would have to work for the fire department.

"You wouldn't catch me working for a private company," Tim said as a matter of fact.

"Not everyone has an in at a firehouse, boyfriend," I teased. "Besides, I never ever want to run into a burning building."

That was true. I only envisioned the idea of working on an ambulance due to the bombing. I never considered being a firefighter.

"Well, I still have to go to Fire One and Fire Two but my dad said the fire department would pay for the training," he replied smiling from ear to ear.

I heard the eagerness in his voice and saw how he glowed when he talked of working there. Of course, where else would he work?

"I have a great deal of respect for you boys that want to be heroes," I noted. "I want to help people but not in a burning building. You can rescue them and I'll take care of their burns."

Our relationship seemed to evolve every day. Tim seemed to have unending patience with me, I enjoyed being around him and now we were both paramedics. What more could I ask for? I wondered.

I applied with EMSA and within a couple of weeks, we both had interviews but for different companies. For me, it was almost like being in school again. I was required to take a written test as well as run a mile under twenty minutes. The next test was agility. Bricks were placed on a stretcher and together with another new person we had to walk up and down a set of bleachers to prove that we could handle ourselves. Happily, I passed.

Tim told me he underwent a similar test only he had to perform a timed Candidate Physical Ability Test. He was also required to run around with a hose, and climb up

and down a ladder holding a dummy with his fire gear on. Of course, he passed too. I knew he would.

With our new jobs came an entirely different set of working hours making it a challenge to see each other as often as we wished. He worked the A B C Kelly shift, which meant he was on 24 hours, off 24, on 24, off 24 on 24 and then 96 hours off. My hours were on 24 hours and off 48. It was not easy to enjoy a day off together without one of us needing some sleep. Tim grew more anxious to marry me so we could at least live in the same house and be there for each other whenever possible. Over time, he wore me down. I admit that I was falling in love with him. He made me feel safe, secure and happy.

To celebrate our new jobs we went to our favorite restaurant. The night was filled with small talk, nothing out of the ordinary. We ate and then enjoyed our game afterward with the fortune cookies. He picked up the cookies and placed one in my hand.

"Quick, open it up," I pressed like an over zealous child. "Tell me your fortune."

"You first," he laughed.

"But you always open yours first," I replied grinning.

"So let's change the routine. You open yours first."

I cracked open the cookie, pulled out the paper and began reading.

"Will you marry me?" I read aloud. Stunned, I re-read the words and tried to take them in. What kind of fortune is this? I wondered.

"Will you marry me?" Tim asked quickly kneeling beside me.

He held a sparkling ring out toward me. I did not have time to think. I was so moved by his ingenuity and without hesitation I hollered, "Yes!" I grabbed him, planted a passionate kiss on his lips and smiled teary eyed. Then he placed the diamond ring on my finger.

"Thank you," he said showing that smile with the chipped tooth that I had grown to love. "I am the happiest man alive!"

I made Tim take me back home so I could tell Lynn and Jessica the good news. They screamed and yelled mixed with hugs, kisses and tears. Next I called my mother.

"Mom!" I said with obvious excitement.

"Is everything all right?" she asked since she mostly did the calling.

"Yes it is. In fact, it's perfect." I said dreamily.

"Well, you sound giddy. Are you calling me to tell me you're in love?"

My mother was a smart woman and she always seemed to be one step ahead of me.

"Mom, I'm going to get married," I announced and it went silent on the other end.

"Mom, you there?"

"Honey, is it Tim?" she asked in a concerned voice. I did not expect this response. It was completely different from the girls.

"Yes!" I shouted undeterred. "He was so romantic, mom. He put the words 'will you marry me' in a fortune cookie. You should see my ring." I sat with my left hand in front of me admiring the shimmering diamond.

"Are you sure?" she asked.

I could not understand why she sounded less than thrilled with the news.

"Yes, I'm sure," I affirmed. "You don't sound very happy for me?"

"Of course, I'm happy for you, sweetie. I just don't want you to make a rash decision. It wasn't that long ago you thought you were in love with Aaron."

That was the last thing I wanted to hear and did not know what to say. I admit that I was angry with her for saying that, even though I knew she was right. It was quiet while both of us gathered our thoughts. I really wanted her to be happy for me. It seemed like a long time before either one of us spoke. Finally, mom broke the silence.

"I hope you plan to get married in Lawton," she said with more of a bounce in her voice.

I decided to put aside her concern when I heard the pleasant ring to her tone. I was so happy and did not want anyone or anything to bring me down.

"Of course, mom."

She seemed to dismiss her fears at that moment and could not wait to begin wedding plans. She reminded me of the small size of Lawton and said she would get started on the guest list. I told her I would love to get married at Mount Scott since that was where most of my fond memories growing up with her had been and she loved that idea. She decided to hold the reception at her house and already knew whom she wanted as the caterer.

Chapter 27
A Serious Accident

My first week at EMSA seemed intimidating. I had heard that some people newly out of paramedic school acquired something called the God syndrome. They thought they were smarter than everyone else but in reality, they knew just enough to get themselves in trouble.

Well, my medic preceptor had this syndrome. His name was Steve and he demonstrated the egoistical attitude that he was an expert who knew even more than the nurses and doctors.

I observed him when we attended at a nursing home to pick up a patient and saw how rude he talked to the nurses and staff. As well, he had little patience with the elderly folks diagnosed with dementia or Alzheimer's who were often confused. He complained that he should not be on such calls. He told me his skills were meant for life-saving circumstances, not dealing with old people driving them to and from hospitals. However, when we attended at an emergency call, his skills were evident. He performed with great knowledge and got the job done.

It was an exhilarating week for me. We had duties every morning and rushed to finish them before our first call. These included stocking and washing our ambulance. Since we stayed at the station for twenty-four hours, we lived in an apartment and everyday chores had to be kept up to maintain cleanliness. Our calls ranged from taking someone from the hospital to a nursing home to car accidents, diabetic emergencies, respiratory

distress and even heart attacks. Whenever we received a Code Three, which meant we must use the lights and sirens, the guys I rode with blasted the volume on the car radio. As a good song peeled out, our adrenalin rose and we jammed to the music. They did not do things like this during my ride-alongs in school but now that I was officially working, I could clearly see the difference.

I learned to inhale my food since most times when we sat to eat the alarm went off. We had to run leaving our food behind to get cold. But the hardest part to me seemed to be nighttime. We turned out the lights to sleep but my mind would not shut off. As well, the bed did not feel like mine and I was not comfortable sleeping in the same room with the men. Then just as I fell asleep, the alarm would peel again and we'd run to the ambulance.

One night we responded to a traffic accident. With help from the firefighters, we got our patient off to the hospital and finished our paperwork. Then we drove back to the station and hopped into bed again. The guys I was precepting with amazed me because they could fall right back to sleep with no problem. I knew this was going to be a learning experience and hopefully in time, I would learn to do the same. Until then, I would go home and crash after my shifts.

After a week I had my own truck and a steady EMT-B partner to work with. Jose had been doing this job for a couple of years and it was a comfort to work with someone who was experienced. Our day began slowly, washing our rig and stocking up supplies inside the truck. Then we took on our house chores. I cleaned the apartment's bathrooms while he vacuumed the floors. I

listened to the radio – waiting - anticipating a call. Jose laughed at me, telling me that soon enough, I would be happy to enjoy the slow times.

A Code Three came through at 9 a.m. for a person slumped over at Walgreens - my first life-saving call. This was just too exciting! We arrived with a fire truck and the six of us rushed inside the store to find our patient. We found a man, probably in his 30's against the wall on the floor. His skin was pale, his eyes were closed and his breathing was slow. We took vitals and blood sugar, which read thirty. After inserting an IV and giving him some D-50, he instantly woke up and asked what happened. He told us that he had a history of being diabetic and took his insulin but forgot to eat breakfast. Since that was not unusual for him, he refused to go to the hospital with us. Okay, this was not really a life-saving call but we did help him and that was all I needed.

The day went on with calls that included picking up an 80-year-old patient that had abnormal lab results, an 8-year-old girl with asthma who could not breathe and a 50-year-old male with chest pains. It was wonderful to be able to use my skills and play detective as I analyzed how I could help. What a feeling of satisfaction to finally do what I had hoped for in life.

Before I went to bed that night, I checked out the moon. According to rumor when the moon was full all the crazies came out and a lot of babies were born. This night would be a test as to whether the rumor was true.

The clock struck 2 a.m. when we got the Code Three for a car accident. We could see the colored flashing

lights a few blocks away. With lights and sirens blasting, we arrived at the scene with two other ambulances and a couple of fire trucks. It appeared that three cars had crashed. A jeep station wagon was traveling north on Shields Boulevard when it collided with a Dodge pick-up truck traveling east on SE 89th Street. There was a stop sign for northbound traffic at the SE 89th St intersection. After the initial collision, the pick-up truck crossed into the westbound land and hit an Oldsmobile station wagon traveling west. The truck sat on its side, the jeep station wagon was crushed on the right side, and the station wagon's hood and windshield were smashed.

Police officers quickly placed flares on the road while the fire chief assessed the scene. It resembled chaos with all the emergency vehicle lights, and people running around yelling and screaming. Firefighters engaged everywhere along with EMTs to make sure the wounded were attended to and everyone in the accident was safe.

The woman who drove the jeep was awake but her head was bleeding from hitting the windshield and she cried in pain.

"I can't feel my legs," she moaned.

A crew took her carefully out of her car, placed her on a backboard with a c-collar and packaged her for the hospital. The man in the station wagon seemed anxious about what happened but escaped with only a few cuts and bruises. The firefighters tried convincing him to go to the hospital but he refused.

It took three firefighters and the Jaws of Life to get a third person out of the pick-up truck. The man was unconsciousness and his breathing was shallow. His face

was swollen and covered with blood. We cautiously slid him out of his vehicle, placed him on a backboard and took his vitals. His right arm was in an awkward position, definitely broken and a ring on his chest resembled the steering wheel. His left leg was amputated under the knee but had a smooth line indicating that it was not a new injury. Setting the gurney in the ambulance, we raced to the hospital. I had a couple of medic firefighters working with me in the back of the ambulance. Oxygen, IV, ECG monitor - this started out textbook until…

"He stopped breathing," yelled a brown-haired firefighter.

I grabbed a BVM and began bagging him with one hundred percent oxygen.

"What does the cardiac monitor say?" I asked.

"His heart is only beating forty times a minute," yelled a blond-haired firefighter.

"Check to see if he has a pulse."

I stopped bagging him for a moment and placed my fingers on his throat.

"No pulse!" I yelled. "PEA," meaning pulseless electrical activity. I became a little flustered but knew I had to perform to the best of my ability if we were to save the man - the reason why I wanted to be a medic in the first place. This was not school where a mistake could be forgiven. This was real life – and possibly death. I surprised myself as I quickly remembered the algorithms, which I applied.

Quickly, I gave the bag valve mask to the brown-haired firefighter and opened the drug box. The blond-haired one began chest compressions. Picking up the epinephrine, I opened the medication and pushed the fluid through the IV. They did CPR for a few more minutes before I asked them to stop and touched his neck again hoping for better results.

"Got a pulse!" I yelled as our ambulance pulled up in front of the hospital.

We ran inside with him and found a team of nurses waiting for us. The brown-haired firefighter never quit bagging this patient giving him much-needed oxygen and the doctor immediately intubated the man. We then submitted our oral report and let the hospital staff to do their jobs.

The hospital seemed busy that night. Three other ambulances had just dropped off patients and the waiting room was packed with people. The emergency rooms were so full that people were lying on beds in the hallways. I found out a couple of women were in labor as well, which all seemed to confirm the rumor about a full moon. I sat in the EMS room to complete my paperwork and realized that I did not have the patient's name or age. I ran to his room where they had already undressed him, scavenged through his clothes for identification and admitted him.

I caught a glimpse of the defenseless man lying in the bed with a tube in his mouth and the vent on breathing for him. The cardiac monitor beeped at a fifty-three beats per minute and the blood pressure cuff was programmed to take a reading every five minutes. His

body seemed lifeless; his face dirty, pale and covered in blood. They gave me a fact sheet, and I waited until I wrote down my vitals and what we had done in the ambulance before I checked the information to copy for my report. I scanned the paper lying in front of me. As I wrote down the name, my hand stopped and the pen fell to the floor. Slowly, I picked up the paper and re-read it.

My chest immediately constricted and began to hurt. I tried to breathe but as much as I tried, I could not and for a brief moment, I panicked. Then I sat down and lowered my head between my legs. I managed a few short inhalations but still could not control my breathing. Tears filled my eyes as I desperately struggled for air. I scampered to the bathroom, shut and locked the door, and then ran to the sink to splash water on my face. I lowered my head again managing to take in a few short and quick breaths. With each forced inhale, my chest heaved and my throat hurt. By this time, I sobbed uncontrollably, which must have been overheard because someone tapped on the bathroom door.

"Are you all right in there?" a voice asked but I could not answer.

I had to regain control of myself. I closed my eyes and paced in circles to slow down my breathing and recapture my composure. Wiping my face, I finally got the courage to return to the EMS room to finish my paperwork. I knew this would be a long night and did not expect to sleep.

Chapter 28
A Time For Tears

The next morning when I finished my shift, I hurried home to take a shower with intentions of returning to the hospital. Tim called asking me about work and I told him about the patients I took care of as well as the terrible car accident. He heard how my voice trembled and warned me not to take my work home with me. He was going on shift and I promised that I would try to come to the firehouse for dinner.

After my shower, I glanced in the mirror. A worn and tired reflection stared back at me. I guess that was the result of going over twenty-four hours without sleep. Patting some preparation H under my eyes and putting on a little makeup, I left the house and drove to a diner across from the hospital to order some coffee and toast. The images of the car accident and my patient kept flashing before my eyes. I had no idea who my patient was while I did my job, just as I was taught. I relived the devastation all around me with the unconscious man, bruised and bleeding, one leg amputated and everything I did to save him.

At 9 a.m., I strolled into the hospital and asked for the name from my run sheet. I was told that he was in the intensive care unit. With all the courage I could gather, I took the elevator to the third floor. When I entered the man's room, he still lay lifeless with his eyes closed but appeared to display a little more color in his face. To me, he seemed better. He was not on ventilation anymore and

the tube was out of his mouth. Someone had cleaned his face but his eyes were swollen from extensive bruising.

The man standing next to him glanced up at me with appreciation in his eyes. I felt a rush of emotion go through my body when he smiled at me.

"Hi Annette," said the familiar voice.

"Hi Tom," I replied and moved to give him a hug. "How's he doing?"

"A lot better," he stated in a weary voice. "They said his heart stopped and he was intubated but he seems to be coming out of the woods." Tired lines drawn on Tom's face showed he had aged.

"I know," I said sadly. "I was the paramedic who took care of him."

"You're a paramedic? He never told me. He did say you were going to EMT school but I never heard anything after that."

"I haven't heard from him in a long time, Tom. I'm not sure he knows."

Tom nodded and turned his face toward the window. We could see the parking lot but not much else.

"Come for a walk with me," he urged. "There's something you need to know." He turned to his son, bent over and kissed him on the cheek before we left the room. I let him lead the way along the hall to the elevator and down to the first floor where we entered the cafeteria.

"You hungry?" he asked as he got himself a tray. "I haven't eaten yet today. I got the phone call at 4 a.m. and came straight here. He hasn't woken up yet but I want to be there when he does."

I couldn't help smiling. One of the things I liked about this man was his compassion. I remembered the story Aaron told me of how Tom lived at the hospital when his mom was ill until the day she died. How hard this must be for him now, knowing his son almost died as well. Tom picked up some scrambled eggs and toast, while I grabbed a bowl of fruit.

"You noticed his leg, eh?" he said between bites and I nodded.

"Unfortunately, he was sent home early with an honorable discharge, which devastated him. He wouldn't call you. He told me he did not want you to see him without his leg because you deserved better. He said he wasn't the man he used to be anymore and wanted you to remember him for who he had been."

Intense anger rose up inside of me. How dare he make choices for me? How dare he break my heart for purely selfish reasons? Even so, I kept my expression steady.

"You still love him, don't you?" Tom asked exploring my face.

"It's complicated," I said showing him my engagement ring

I let my hand slowly drift back to the table. Tom covered my hand with his and gave it a gentle pat.

"It's all right, Annette. You didn't know if he was around or even alive."

Frustration appeared on his face as he continued.

"I told him to call you but you know how stubborn he could be at times."

Tears formed in my eyes and I tried to blink them away. All I could do at that point was be angry with myself. I knew I should have contacted his father and asked how Aaron was but I didn't. I made plenty of excuses and never got around to it. I watched as Tom pulled a wrinkled letter from his pocket.

"I want you to read this letter. I've carried it around with me like a crazy man hoping some day I would bump into you but I never believed that day would come." He slid the envelope across the table toward me. A tear slipped down my cheek as I stared at it. I was almost too afraid to pick it up.

"Go on, take it," he urged. "I need to get back to my son's room." Tom stood up, pushed the chair back under the table and picked up his empty tray.

"It was good to see you, Annette. Thanks for taking care of my boy."

As I peered up at him, a few more tears splashed down my cheeks. He nodded and smiled with obvious gratitude before walking away. I sat for a few more minutes staring at the envelope. Finally, I got the courage to pick it up and walked out to my car. Not sure where I should go, I drove until I found myself at the pond where Aaron and I used to feed the ducks - the one where we made out like teenagers - the one I had not returned to since the last time he was with me.

I had no bread for the ducks so I made my way to the picnic table, climbed up the bench and sat on top. I slipped the envelope out of my pocket and slowly

withdrew the letter. I sensed at that moment that I would need to be strong.

Dear Dad,

I finally got my taste of real combat with bombs, missiles and mortars exploding for a few days. My squad was assigned to an outlying neighborhood to clear out the enemy. We went from house to house only to see the charred remains of a truck or a lifeless body in a house. While we patrolled, civilians occasionally rushed out to us with their arms up asking for help with sporadic rifle fire in the air making us alert to the Taliban waiting for us.

Wouldn't you know it; we were assaulted by heavy fire coming from a building up the street. We tried to take cover and slip through the shooting gallery to a safer spot on the other side of the road. When we got to the other side, we shot thousands of rounds into the enemy's position. We waited until it was safe and moved cautiously to the building. One of the men threw a grenade to blast open the front door. The smoke was heavy and sulfur hung in the air.

Once we got inside and close the door, the enemy started shooting from a crawl space beneath the floor. We responded with hundreds of rounds. Chips of plaster, brick and wood flew as the walls were decimated. We ran outside and one of the boys stepped on what he thought was a rock. It was actually a landmine and it exploded, killing that soldier. Pieces of the shrapnel hit my leg leaving me in so much pain. They wrapped my leg and carried me back to base. When the gunfire finally quit, there was a strange

quietness, except for the ringing in my ears and the guys cussing about their experience.

Dad, I never felt pain like I did that day. When I finally looked at my leg, I realized that my foot was missing. I passed out and am not sure for how long but I woke up in the infirmary. The doctors had to amputate below my knee. They said they couldn't save my foot and they were sending me home. I will write to let you know when to pick me up. It will be a while.

Meanwhile, don't say anything to Annette. I don't want her to see me like this. What kind of life could she share with a cripple? I have every letter she wrote but I quit writing back to make her think I didn't care for her anymore. Hopefully, she will move on. I love her too much, so I need to spare her from this pain.

Write to you soon, dad.

Love, Aaron

My mind flashed back to the past and my body flooded with intense emotions. I was not sure how to take Aaron's decision. Was it a selfish or a heroic act? Why didn't he consult me about my feelings and ask me if I wanted out. Maybe he thought I would stay for pity and he did not want that. Does he have any idea how much he hurt me? I wondered.

My mind worked on overdrive trying to understand. He had no idea how many tears I shed for him each time I went to the mailbox hoping and praying but not receiving a letter. I needed something, even if I had to read the words, "I don't love you anymore." I needed to know he was all right. I remembered praying to God,

asking Him to watch over Aaron, to keep him safe and bring him home to me. I could not understand why God did not answer my prayers.

I became so depressed that I dove headlong into paramedic school making my classes my life. I had to forget about life, as I knew it. I had to stay busy. Whenever a student complained about school taking up too much of his life, I just smiled, happy that I was too preoccupied to think of anything else. Then of course, my other distraction became Tim – sweet and handsome Tim. He hung around me like a moth to a light even though I give him no reason to be so kind.

Over time, I had come to the conclusion that Aaron and I were finished. He did not seem like the kind of man to just turn and run from a bad situation - or was he? Aaron originally joined the army because his dad quit communicating with him after his mother's death. I knew he also wanted to join for our country and hoped his dad would be proud of him but maybe, just maybe, he was also running away from his life. Was I so much in love that I was too blind to recognize it? It took so long before my mind and heart would allow me to smile again. Thank heavens for Tim listening to me when I cried over Aaron, holding me and letting me vent. He has such a gentleman, never taking advantage of me, although he might easily have done so.

I had promised to visit Tim at the firehouse for dinner but really did not feel up to it. The problem was what to tell him. How could I say Aaron was back in town?

"Um… Tim, remember the boyfriend I told you about in the army who quit writing to me? Well, he is the one I rescued last night."

I knew that would not go over well. I jumped down from the picnic table and hurried to my car. I felt so run down and hoped I could find a way to get out of seeing Tim – at least that day. I desperately needed time to myself but was so tired that I wondered how I could even think straight. I finally decided that I should drive to the firehouse to talk to Tim. When I arrived, the fire truck sat in the garage so I knew he was there. I walked in with hellos to the boys before he noticed me.

"To what do I owe this surprise?" he asked smiling.

Tim put his arms around me and drew me close before kissing my lips. I did not kiss him back with the same passion I usually displayed.

"What's wrong?" Tim asked pulling away.

"I'm so tired, Tim," I began, which was not a lie.

"Didn't you sleep when you got home this morning?" he responded looking confused.

"No. I went back to the hospital to check up on my patient from last night."

I did not have the courage to tell him who my patient was yet. Tim closed his eyes and shook his head.

"What did I tell you about getting too involved with your patients?" he said pulling me close again. "So why are you here now instead of sleeping?"

"I'm not sure," I confessed. "I guess to say I might not see you for dinner tonight."

"It's okay," he replied smiling. "I understand." But then pouting, he added, "Please don't make a habit of this. I really miss you, you know."

"I miss you too," I said and really meant it.

"Fine, go home and go to bed," he said kissing my forehead. "You can owe me later."

Tim winked and I walked out knowing he was watching me. I went straight home and into my bedroom. I had no energy to sit, eat or even turn on the television. However, I decided to take a shower so the hot water would sooth my aching body. As well, I had a headache and my ears were ringing.

I stood under the shower letting the water flow over my head, into my eyes and over my body. The magic of the steaming water helped me relax… so much so that I felt a strange release and started to cry. It began softly and I wondered why. Then the tension of the day took over and I sobbed irrepressibly until I found myself sitting in the bathtub under the still-running shower. I was not sure if I got wetter from my tears or the water from the showerhead. I do not remember how long I sat in the tub but the water eventually turned cold.

Once I stepped out and dried off, I looked into the steamed mirror. My reflection revealed eyes that were bloodshot and puffy. Quickly, I put on a pair of pajamas and lay back in bed. The tears continued to flow but I could not tell if they were angry or sorry tears.

Chapter 29
Memories, Memories

At 11 a.m., there was a knock on my bedroom door. I tried to ignore the sound but it persisted.

"Go away," I yelled from under my covers.

"You decent?" Tim's voice replied.

"Ah… yes," I squeaked quietly.

When he opened the door and walked in, a concerned expression covered his face.

"I tried calling you last night but your roommates said you were sleeping. I hadn't heard from you yet today, so I got worried. Are you okay?"

Tim sat next to me on the bed and laid his hand on my waist, which was under the covers.

"I'm fine," I answered weakly. What's wrong with me? I wondered taking in his handsome features. Here's a man who actually worries about me and I'm crying about someone in my past that doesn't care.

Tim leaned down and kissed me softly.

"Get dressed," he urged smiling. "Let's do something today."

When he left the room, I got up and splashed some water on my face. As I dressed, I glanced down at my engagement ring. Memories of the day he asked me to marry him flashed into my mind. I recalled how much time and imagination he put into his scheme to have me open the fortune cookie with the right words inside. It was so romantic. The love and laugher we shared put a smile back on my face. I needed that.

I do love this man, I thought. If I didn't, I'd never have accepted his ring. Angry with myself, I determined to forget about the accident and the fact that Aaron was home. I would simply believe he went on without me so I could live happily ever after with Tim. I had to convince myself of that.

The rest of the day with Tim was wonderful as I set aside all thoughts of Aaron. We went to the movies and out to eat, laughing, talking and enjoying each other's company. I loved holding his hand and spending time with him but when he tried to make out in his car, I felt queasy. I did not think he was aware it though. I tried to hide my uneasiness and kissed him with as much love and passion as I had in the past.

I decided that as usual, I would throw myself into my work. I needed time to forget, time to forgive and time to let go. I never went back to the hospital again to check on Aaron.

The following month seemed to drift by slowly. I worked on the ambulance as much as I was allowed. I pulled so many shifts that Tim got upset about all the overtime. However, I convinced him that I needed the money for things like a wedding dress and shoes, and presents for my bridesmaids. I loved my work but deep down I knew I was doing more of it to avoid thinking about Aaron. I wished that I had not attended at the car accident that night. Then I would not have this awful weight on my shoulders.

I retraced everything in my mind. I told myself over and over that he made the decision to stop writing as well as the conclusion that I would not be able to deal with his infirmity. Yet the words from his father always crept in. He did not want to be a bother to me as a cripple. He thought I deserved more than that even though he still loved me.

Meanwhile, my life entered a new phase. I attended paramedic school, received my certificate and was then able to make a difference in people's lives. Along the way, I found a man with the same interest and without even trying I fell in love.

Ugh, so why is this so hard for me? I wondered knowing that I still felt something for Aaron. Is it possible to be in love with two people at the same time?

Part of me wondered if I should visit Aaron again to see if the spark between us was still alive. The other part of me disagreed. After all, he had not been around and I was happy once I got him out of my system.

You found someone who is head over heels in love with you, I thought. Think about that!

I knew I loved Tim but my feelings were different than they were before. With Aaron, I fell for him the first time I saw him. With Tim, my love had to grow.

Over the following weeks, work did its part to keep me busy bringing sick people to hospitals and there were more car accidents than usual or so it seemed. Often, we did not even have time to eat with calls interrupting our meals. I lost weight and Tim grew concerned.

"Are you sick?" he asked one day. "You look too thin."

Of course, I told him I was fine and tried to be extra nice when I did get the chance to see him. I said things like, "I don't deserve you." He only laughed, looked into my eyes and reminded me of how much he loved me. Instead of spending my days thinking about Aaron, I focused instead on how much I loved Tim. I often gazed at the beautiful diamond he placed on my finger. That was reality and my heart fluttered at the thought. On nights that I did not work, which seemed to be few and far between, I was so tired and my bed beckoned me.

At the end of the month, I received a call from Judy at the beauty salon around 9 a.m. She said someone made an appointment with me and wondered if I could come in right away. Although it was my day off, I had no plans. I did not pick up overtime with the ambulance but still wanted to keep occupied so I told her I would be in by 11 a.m. I drove to the salon and peered through the glass front door. I could see Judy at her desk talking on the phone.

I opened the door to the familiar smell of perm solution, which brought back so many fond memories. As I walked toward my station, Betty and Veronica bombarded me with chipper hellos and hugs. After a few pleasantries, my eyes shifted to my chair and I immediately recognized the back of his head, only his hair seemed a bit longer falling past the collar of his shirt. He caught sight of me through the mirror and swung the chair around. I visually examined his body with the muscular chest and arms, which were so familiar. He wore shorts, which revealed his amputated

left leg. Then realization struck me. It was the first time I had seen Aaron awake, alert and alive. Our eyes locked.

"Hello Annette," he called in a dreamy voice.

My heart stopped, just like the first time we met and I could not help being drawn to him.

"What are you doing here, Aaron?" I replied, quickly becoming aware of the angst in my voice.

"We need to talk."

An awkward silence hovered over us as we stared at each other. I was amazed that I managed to maintain my composure without an anxiety attack. Aaron reached over to grab his crutch, which leaned against my station. I immediately reacted and walked over to pick it up for him.

"No!" he demanded.

Betty, Veronica, and Judy stopped what they were doing and looked our way. I moved back and watched him use his left arm to set the crutch straight on the floor as he put pressure on his right leg. I tried to slip my hand under his right arm to help him get up.

"I can do this myself," he said in a stern voice. He stepped on his right leg and pushed himself up. Then he placed the crutch under his left arm and stood up. I could see the anger in his face reflecting the unwanted reward he received while helping our country. His discontent with his new way of life was painfully visible.

Do I even know him anymore? I wondered.

"Will you take a ride with me?" Aaron asked interrupting the thought.

"Sure."

I could see Judy shaking her head so I told her I would be fine before following him out of the salon. I was afraid to grab the door for him. He opened it and even held it for me to exit ahead of him. At his car, he opened my door first and by the time I got in, he was already at the driver's side. He hesitated for a minute as if he did not know what to do with his crutch but then placed it on the back seat. I must have had one of my odd expressions on my face.

"I don't need my left leg to drive a car," he said firmly.

I tried not to stare as he put his foot on the gas pedal. I was definitely a little apprehensive about this trip. I did not know why he came to the salon or where we were going. Aaron turned the radio on while I stared out the passenger window with my arms crossed.

Why am I here? I wondered and then Tim came to mind. I should be spending my time with him.

We drove for nearly twenty minutes before Aaron spoke.

"Annette," he said lowering the radio volume, "you must be wondering why I want to talk to you."

"Yes, of course."

He quickly looked at me and flashed a small smile before turning his face back to the road. This made me feel a little more comfortable

"I want to thank you for saving my life," he said with precise pronunciation of each word. "I know you have a lot of things you might want to ask me… and I know I owe you a big explanation."

I relaxed a little letting my arms fall to my lap.

"My dad told me he talked with you at the hospital and that you were the one who pulled me out of the car."

"I wasn't the only one," I said interrupting him. "There was a team of us who work together. Your car sat on its side. They actually used the Jaws of Life to get you out. Two other cars were involved and another woman went to the hospital too. I was worried about you because you stopped breathing… and then your heart…" I had to stop talking to take a deep breath.

"This must be hard on you," Aaron said. "What a way for you to see me after such a long time."

"I had no idea who I was working on," I said glaring at him. "Your face was all swollen and bloody, and you were missing part of a leg."

My eyes shifted to his amputation and I noticed how his knee just sort of stood up on the seat. Embarrassed, I stared straight ahead.

"You were just another patient but when I got the paperwork and read your name, I had an anxiety attack." My body started to shake as I relived the experience.

"Why are you here, Aaron?"

He squirmed in his seat looking a little uncomfortable.

"I need to explain why I quit writing, Annette. First, I want you to know that I still love you very much and I needed your letters to survive," he explained and his tone became more harsh as he continued. "Our orders were to help the innocent civilians. The fighting seemed sporadic at first. The Taliban forces decided to hang onto Kabul because they wanted to make Afghanistan the world's purest Islamic state. Then this extremist group

introduced a bloody wave of killings and amputations. We tried to help the wounded and carry them out of danger. One afternoon, we were walking back home when all of a sudden, we were surrounded by heavy gunfire coming from a building down the street." Aaron stopped for a second and glanced at me.

"You read the letter I wrote to my dad so I don't really have to relive that day. The screaming and yelling along with the heavy artillery was enough to make anyone deaf. I saw my friend die when he stepped on the mine and tried to run but the shrapnel hit my leg and I flew to the ground. When the firing stopped, I thought for sure no one but me had survived. After the smoke cleared, there was this awful quiet. My ears started ringing when a couple of guys grabbed my arms to help me up. That was when I caught a glimpse of my leg. My foot seemed to be dangling and then the pain took over – the worst pain I ever had. As they tried to wrap my leg, they gave me morphine and I passed out. I don't know how long I was unconscious but when I came to, I was lying in a hospital bed - white sheets on me and confused. I forgot about what happened and thought I could get up. I could not believe my eyes when I tried to move my legs and saw part of my left leg missing. I had to go through rehab to help me with my balance and learn how to walk with a crutch."

Aaron's voice sounded sad as he related the final part. "I haven't been home all that long now and I'm not in the service anymore."

I peered up at him. His story was terrible but it did not explain why he stopped writing to me. As we drove, I began to acknowledge familiar surroundings. He had brought me to the woods - the same ones where we fished on our first date. Hearing the gravel crackle under the tires seemed oddly comforting.

"Let's go for a walk," he suggested, "but this time, I need your help. I usually put my crutch in the front seat so I can grab it, so if you don't mind."

My eyes scanned his face before I reached over the seat and passed him his crutch.

"Thank you," he whispered.

Aaron did not seem to have the hang of the crutch yet but he flashed a smile and took the lead. We walked silently toward the stream like we did so long ago only his walk was more of a hop. We followed the stream toward the big rocks where the little waterfall began but this time, we did not go further. Aaron looked at me with a dejected expression.

"I can't go this way anymore. I need two legs to climb the rocks and fight the rolling water."

He quickly let his eyes fall to his missing foot before lifting his face back to me. "Do you understand yet, why I quit writing?"

Tears filled my eyes as I admired this poor defensive man.

"No!" I yelled at him and stomped off toward the car.

Aaron tried to hobble along behind me.

"There must be another way to get to your fishing spot," I said stubbornly standing with my legs apart and

my arms folded across my chest. "Why are you giving up so easily?"

"Look at me, Annette," his voice growing louder. "I am not the same man you knew. I can't go with you on your hikes at Mount Scott either. I am a cripple."

"You've changed, Aaron," I replied tears rolling down my cheeks. "You used to be excited with life, with the wilderness and with me. Now, I don't even know who you are." I stopped and shook my head in disgust. "You are alive aren't you? Isn't that enough to be thankful for?"

"You have no idea what you're talking about," he replied, his body tense with rage. "You don't understand what it's like not knowing how to get up in the middle of the night without a crutch. To realize that you're not the same physically or what it's like to have people stare at you for your misfortune - pitying you."

"Is that what you think?" I cried. "I think you're a charity case?"

I watched him hobble to a nearby picnic table, sit on the bench and drop his face into his hands. As tension built in the air, neither of us said a word. I slowly dragged my feet to the picnic table and sat across from him. He seemed to be crying so I leaned forward and gave his hand a little squeeze. He nodded and wiped his face with his hands before he spoke again.

"How are you doing, Annette?"

"I'm quite well."

Aaron noticed the ring on my left hand and I quickly withdrew it from the table.

"No don't," he said as he brought his hands together. "When did it start with him?"

"I don't know for sure. This may sound crazy but it didn't happen like you might think. It wasn't as if I planned on getting engaged," I sighed aloud. "This happened a couple of months ago while I was going to paramedic school. Remember I told you that I wanted to be a paramedic after the bombing? This guy was one of the students in the class."

I stopped for a moment and leaned in toward him.

"Paramedic school was really tough and I actually studied at Denny's Restaurant so no one would disturb me. He started showing up and later became my study partner. We never talked about anything but school. There was so much to learn, and along with clinical and still working, we really didn't have any life to talk about." I drew circles on the table with my fingers as I continued. "Anyway, we spent a lot of time together and he was good at consoling me whenever I seemed down and explaining things I didn't understand. Well, you stopped writing to me, Aaron. I never told him about you. I also never acted as if I liked him. We were just study partners and I never let on that I was interested in anyone or anything but school. It was when we had to study for our National Registry test that I finally talked about you. He encouraged me and told me to think positively. I needed to finally talk to somebody and he was there for me. We helped each other and passed the exam. After that, he let me know how he felt about me. Little by little, I guess we fell in love."

Aaron's eyes met mine.

"I didn't want to fall in love again. Do you have any idea how hurt I felt because you quite writing me?"

He offered no answer. We sat quietly for a while before I glanced at my wristwatch and realized that it was getting late.

"Aaron," I whispered. "I need to go home now."

He nodded and I followed him to the car. Before we drove off, his eyes caught mine.

"Thanks for coming with me today," he said. "Seeing you made a world of difference. I never should have stopped writing. I hope you will forgive me."

As his eyes stared into mine, memories of the past rushed back and for a brief moment I felt every emotion, every hope and dream I'd ever had for us. Aaron drove me home in silence but I felt strongly aware of him next to me. When we reached my house, he parked on the street.

"You know," he said turning toward me, "each day I wake up nervous and tense, and bitter and frustrated over the man I've become. I needed someone to talk to."

I was not sure what he wanted me to say but he took my hand and gently squeezed it before letting go.

"Well, it was great seeing you," I replied smiling.

As I opened the car door, Aaron leaned toward me. "Hey, can I take you someplace tomorrow?"

"Sure, what time?" I responded without thinking.

"Pick you up at nine."

I stumbled into the house, said hey to my roommates and could sense their stares but I was not in the mood to talk yet.

"Tim called a couple of times tonight," Lynn said as she studied my face. "Where have you been?"

"Out," I replied bluntly before picking up the phone to call Tim back. "Tim, it's me."

I walked in circles not knowing what I should say. Since the room fell quiet, I realized that Lynn and Jessica were eavesdropping.

"I was wondering where you were," he said naively. "I thought perhaps we could go to a movie and out for Chinese food tomorrow?"

"Can I take a rain check?" I asked meekly. "I need some time to myself."

"Are you getting cold feet?"

"No, silly. I just need some time to think," I replied and the line went quiet for a moment.

"Okay, anything you want to talk about?"

I caught myself shaking my head before I answered.

"No, not really," I replied and after an awkward moment of silence I added, "Night, Tim. I'm going to bed now."

"I love you," he said quickly.

"I love you too. Good night."

I went straight to my room, hot tears burning in the back of my eyes. As I changed into my nightclothes, the tears began to flow. I lay in bed pondering the past and the present. I tried to sleep but images of Aaron - the vision I had of him before he left for the army – usurped any other thoughts. I remembered how happy we were but also how much he had changed. He really wasn't the man I'd known – or thought I'd known – so well.

"Why God, why?" I asked in silent prayer.

Chapter 30
A New Day

In the morning I watched a gorgeous sun come up - a beautiful orange ball that emerged from the horizon. I showered to get ready for the day and found myself excited at the prospect of being with Aaron. Donning jeans and a dark blue sweater, I prepared a cup of coffee and waited anxiously for the doorbell to ring. Aaron was to arrive at 9 a.m., thankfully after my roommates had already gone to school. He was right on time!

"Good morning," I said smiling as I opened the door.

He leaned in and kissed me on the cheek.

"Ready?" he asked offering his arm.

We walked slowly to the car: Aaron, me, and his crutch but he seemed to be in a much better mood than he'd been the day before.

"Where are we going?" I asked curiously.

"You know I like adventures and to take you to interesting places," he replied starting the car. "Those were your words."

I thought of the past and wondered what he had up his sleeve.

"So what are your plans now?" I asked leaning back in my seat.

"What do you mean?"

"You wanted to be in the army full time so now what are you going to do with your life?"

I scanned his face watching his expressions, which seemed to convey confusion.

"I haven't given any thought to my future yet," he shrugged.

"Well why not?"

"I don't know. Guess this is so new to me, not having my leg and I just seem lost, like I don't belong anywhere."

"What about college? You started school once remember? You could go back and find something that interests you - something to make you appreciate life and find self-worth again?"

"Like what?" he questioned.

I thought for a minute. My eyes flashed from him to the passenger window, then to his left leg. When I realized I was staring, I focused back on Aaron's face.

"How about being a school teacher?" I asked and he laughed. "What's so funny about that? Didn't you say once that you'd like to do that?"

"So my students can make fun of me?" he asked, sarcasm clear in his voice.

"What is your problem?" I snapped. "You could help kids by teaching them not to let anything get in their way of their dreams – to make a difference in the world. You could show them that even after you went to war to keep America safe, you still knew life was worth living - that it was possible to go on no matter how overwhelming the situation might seem."

Aaron remained quiet, thinking I supposed. I recalled the first time we met when he had everything figured out with his life.

"A penny for your thoughts?" he said drawing me back to reality.

"I was just thinking how jealous I was when we first met. I had no idea what I wanted to do with my life and you had all the answers."

"Time sure can change things can't it?"

"I'm sorry. I didn't intend to hurt you, Aaron. I just want you to see life more positively."

"I know you didn't mean it, Annette. My dad said you were a keeper, that you would keep me young and alive."

His words made me uncomfortable and I seriously wondered why I chose to go out with him instead of Tim. I looked straight ahead as we drove for a few more miles in silence. When Aaron spotted an oversized sign, he pointed to it.

"See that, Arbuckle Wilderness? That's where we're going."

Again he did his magic, plastering a smile on my face as I anticipated a fascinating day ahead of us. We drove into the park and Aaron paid the entry fee at the gate. Once inside, he gave me some money to purchase cups of food that did not look all that appetizing.

"Is this a zoo?" I asked bewildered as I hopped back into the car.

"Yep, but much different than you've probably ever seen."

We followed a path lined with trees and bushes. All of a sudden, a deer sprinted in front of the car as if we did not exist. Then a donkey strolled by.

"Do you want to feed them?" Aaron asked.

"Yeah!" I replied eagerly and watched as he held one of the cups outside the car window.

A donkey strutted up and ate the food right out of his hand. I felt nervous at first, until I realized that the animals did not intend to hurt us. Soon antelopes and deer trotted over to partake of the feast. After they ate some of the food, we encountered camels, llama and zebras. Like a curious child, I gawked at all the animals we saw along the way.

They were both breathtaking and astonishing! When some ostriches arrived for their share, the other animals left. They seemed intimidated by those long-necked creatures that tried to reach right inside the car. We finally had to close our windows to make them skedaddle.

Up ahead we saw a school bus loaded with children. It had stopped so they could feed a couple of lanky giraffes. How funny it was to watch them stretch their long necks down for the food, and to hear the children giggle and scream with glee. As we drove on, we encountered tigers, rhinos, monkeys and some exotic birds in cages. We never got out of the car but gaped in amazement at everything – the animals and the scenery.

At one spot while feeding some goats, a kid jumped onto the front hood of the car and scampered onto the roof. Aaron moved ever so slowly to see if the kid would jump but he did not budge! We waited patiently while other animals appeared. Then when more ostriches arrived, the kid frantically scurried down.

This excursion took us back in time when the earth's animals could roam freely and the old Aaron seemed to return. Afterward, we stopped at a cafeteria for a bite to eat. I passed him his crutch and carried the trays to our table. Some affable small talk ensued while we ate. Then we drove back to Norman while discussing the outdoor zoo and recalling our astounding adventure.

I thought I was headed home but Aaron pulled into our duck pond and my heart leapt. That was our place. I felt my throat go dry as he parked the car. He turned toward me and his eyes beheld mine. Our previous time together flooded my entire being and the old feelings overwhelmed me. It felt as though I was falling in love with Aaron all over again.

"Why did you quit writing to me?" I blurted out, still seeking a satisfactory answer. "I still loved you. Why did you make up my mind for me and not give me a chance to make such a monumental decision."

Tears fell onto my lap as I struggled to understand and I looked at him longingly.

"I still love you, Annette," he replied moving closer but still not offering a direct answer.

I felt his hand touch the back of my neck as he pulled me toward him. Then his lips found mine. His kiss was inviting and I fervently embraced him. I pushed my body closer to his and he kissed me deeply, quite literally taking my breath away. As he kissed my ear and his tongue explored my neck, I shivered. Then his mouth found mine again.

"You're the best thing that ever happened to me," he whispered.

We kissed a little longer before he whispered again: "You make me feel alive again. I love you, Annette and always will."

We continued to make out in his car and then just held each other. When we met, it was love at first sight. How I

wished to go back in time before life became so complicated.

"I'd better get you home," he said finally.

Darkness had consumed the sky and the moon glistened over the duck pond creating the perfect romantic setting. Our fingers intertwined as we drove out of the park.

"Can I see you tomorrow?" he asked as we pulled up to my house. He flashed that smile with the dimples that I fell in love with so long ago.

"No, I have work tomorrow," I replied sadly.

I did not want him to leave. With a soft kiss goodnight, I scooted from the car and watched him drive away. That night, I went to bed completely confused. What was I doing? Staring at the dark ceiling, I wondered where my heart truly belonged. How could I be in love with two men, I thought with bewilderment.

I closed my eyes and thought of Tim. Would he ever forgive me for spending this time with Aaron?

Chapter 31
Torn Between Two Loves

The alarm jolted me awake before the sun came up so I could get ready for work. It was likely going to be a busy day and for that, I was grateful; I'd have no time to think. When I arrived at work, I checked out my truck and helped clean the apartment. At 9 a.m., a call came in for someone with chest pain. I ran the protocols through my mind as we headed to the scene.

We arrived at a nursing home and found an 80-year-old male with a pacemaker/internal defibrillator. The nurse on staff said the pain began about 3 a.m. and the patient noted that it had a rhythmic beat to it. He was a cute old fellow with a friendly smile but he was clearly frightened so I clasped his hand in mine and coaxed him to relax before taking his vitals. With his help, we transferred him to the gurney, inserted an IV, gave him oxygen, hooked up the ECG leads and headed to the hospital. The man kept his hand over his heart, jumping slightly every time the pain returned. At emergency, the doctor said his defibrillator was misfiring.

I finished my paperwork before we received our next call at 10:30 a.m. It was a 962, which meant a motor vehicle accident again. The fire department truck arrived on scene first. I learned that one car stopped too quickly causing the vehicle behind to slam into its rear. As we

drove up to the scene, several people stood around while the firefighters took vitals.

"Medic 284, you are cancelled," we heard on our radio. It was only a fender bender. As we circled around, I searched the scene. One firefighter glanced up and waved as we drove off. It was Tim.

At 11 a.m., we received a call for a person down at Walgreens. When we arrived, we were promptly escorted to the pharmacy area where a woman was slumped over in a chair. We took her vitals and blood sugar, and my meter indicated that her sugar was low. I quickly put in an IV and slipped some D-50 through the tube. I loved D-50 because it was like a miracle drug. Within seconds, the woman awoke wondering why so many people had gathered around her. We learned she had a history of diabetes. Although she had taken her insulin, she did not have breakfast that day. She would not go to the hospital but promised to eat soon.

When noon rolled around, we stopped at Burger King to pick up some lunch. We brought it back to the station but almost immediately received another 962 call. The burgers would have to wait. We showed up on scene along with firefighters. It was a frightful situation with several police cars on site and officers directing traffic. A driver had lost control of his car and hit a telephone pole. The front of the vehicle was wrapped around the pole and three teenagers were still inside. The windshield resembled a spider web of cracks in the glass.

My partner and I ran to the car first and found the driver's body slumped over, eyes closed. He had no pulse and his head was bleeding profusely. When we opened

his shirt, his chest appeared caved in and bruised. Nervously, I yelled for some firefighters who helped me get him out of the vehicle. Then I began CPR. On the monitor, his pulse was asystole, so I stuck in an IV, continued with CPR and administered epinephrine. We tried our best to revive him but had to call him in the field. Since this was a fatality, the police cordoned off the street so no one else could enter.

I noticed Tim's sad expression as he walked slowly past me.

"It isn't fair," he whispered before joining his team to help the others.

Some of the firefighters concentrated on the two other teenagers. One sat in the front passenger seat with his head bleeding and in shock over what had just happened. While he held his head and complained of pain, he noted that he did not put on his seat belt. They decided to take him out on a backboard. The other teen in the back seat had only minor injuries but hysterically asked about his friends.

Within minutes a dark-haired woman ran up to the scene calling her son's name. A couple of police officers attempted to stop her but she broke through. Rushing to her son's side, she fell on her knees sobbing. A couple of firefighters tried to help her stand but she fought them off and threw herself over the boy's body wailing even louder. She was obviously in great emotional pain and the sound of her cries caused a knot to form in my stomach.

I could not keep watching her so I shifted my eyes towards Tim who decided to help the woman. He slowly dragged his feet as he moved toward her with a look of discontentment. He knelt down beside her and whispered something. The frantic mother glanced at him with grateful eyes and they began to talk. Her desperate whimpers simmered down and after a few more hugs to her son, she leaned on Tim as he helped her stand up. The compassion he showed this woman brought tears to my eyes. Then he took her over to the police who wanted to talk to her. I waited until he was alone before I approached and asked him what he said to her.

"I told her to take her time, that I understood what she was going through because I suffered something like that with my brother. I also said that I would sit with her for as long as she wished."

This call really touched me and the reality of it hit me in the head like a two-by-four. Life was so short and far too precious. We could not take one day for granted. I knew I had to make an important personal decision and it could not wait.

For the rest of the day I struggled inside. Memories of Aaron and falling in love swept over me. I remembered gutting my first fish and sitting in the wilderness as he made dinner. I recalled his face as he took in my world at Mount Scott and the fun we had together. I also remembered our talks at the duck pond and how he shared his inner most feelings with me. Then I thought about the night we made love and I gave him the most intimate part of me. Something I never gave anyone else. Of course the tears began to flow again; I held my chest and sucked in a deep breath. As wonderful as it was, it all seemed like so long ago.

I also relived the agony of not receiving his letters and felt nauseous thinking of the many hours I cried. I recalled the loneliness that crept through my body, mind and soul. Then a mixture of pain, anger and resentment gripped me. I recalled how Tim carried me patiently through those awful times. He was so kind and compassionate with no expectations.

By the time my shift ended, I knew what I had to do. I drove straight to the firehouse to catch Tim before he left work. He looked tired but still handsome as the sun played across his chiseled face.

"Hi," he said when he saw me coming. I could tell by his expression that he knew something was wrong.

"You okay?" he asked, his eyes examining me.

"We need to talk," I said, my voice wavering.

Though I initially offered a fake smile, it quickly disappeared because I was not sure how to tell him that Aaron was back and I'd spent the previous day with him.

"Now?"

I knew I should say something before I chickened out but I just stood wringing my hands.

"Aaron is back." I blurted.

Tim's jaw dropped like he'd just lost his best friend.

"And that means what?"

I lifted my hands over my head while my shoulders went forward but did not respond.

"Come on," he said reaching for my hand. "Let's take a walk."

I followed him to the park behind the firehouse and we walked the path. The sun shone overhead with a few scattered big fluffy clouds floating by. A man walking a barking dog passed by us. As we strode slowly along, I tried to keep my expression steady but I knew Tim could read my face anyway.

"So when did you talk to him?" he asked, his fingers intermingled with mine. The warmth of his hand felt so comfortable, like it belonged there. I could feel my love for him and hated what I had to tell him but I owed him the truth.

"I have seen him the last couple of days, Tim."

I could not stand the way he squirmed yet he said nothing. He still held my hand waiting for me to finish.

"He was the man I saved at the car accident about six weeks ago."

He began to loosen his grip so I closed my fingers around his not wanting to let go. My stomach ached over what I must be doing to him.

"I didn't know at the time until I read the paperwork. Then the next morning, I went to the hospital to see how he was doing. He was still unconsciousness but I did talk to his father."

Reaching into my pocket, I took out the letter Aaron's dad gave me and passed it to Tim. He dropped my hand and stopped walking as he read it. I watched his face tense up while he skimmed the page.

"So he lost his leg in combat. He didn't want you to feel sorry for him so he acted like he didn't care anymore. What a coward. If he was a man," Tim said

with anger evident in his voice, "he would have continued the letters and stayed honest with you. Does he have any idea how much you cried missing him?" He tore the letter in half and let the pieces drop to the ground.

"And I suppose now he wants you back like nothing ever happened. What are you going to do, Annette?"

By that time, he paced almost frantically in circles but did not wait for me to answer.

"You already made up your mind, I'm sure. You have been seeing him."

Then he stopped, grabbed my hand and brought my fingers to his face.

"Doesn't this mean anything to you?"

He pushed my hand back down, let it go and I began to shake. I had never seen him like that and tears spilled down my cheeks. Then he turned his back toward me, placed his hands firmly on his hips and shook his head. I watched his back arch as he took a couple of deep breaths. With his head down, he slowly turned to face me again. I shifted my eyes toward the ground.

"You know I love you, Annette," he said softly. "I shouldn't have to ask you to stay with me." Stopping for a moment he added, "I'll give you some space."

Peeking up from under my bangs, I saw how torn he looked.

"We both worked hard yesterday," he said. "I'm going home to get some sleep." He placed two fingers under my chin and brought my face toward his. His beautiful blue eyes pierced into mine.

"Remember I love you. Talk to you soon…"

With that he turned and walked away. As he did, I heard him whisper under his breath, "I hope."

I immediately broke down. The last thing I wanted was to hurt or upset Tim. I felt like running to him and telling him everything was all right but I knew I had to make up my mind and to do that I also needed to see Aaron again. Picking up the torn letter, I rushed to my car. I was tired – no - totally worn out. After a busy time on the truck the day before, exhaustion had set in and the thought of sleep was most welcome.

Even though it was only 10 a.m., I took a swig of Nyquil to drug myself to sleep. I felt so overtired and had so much on my mind, I was sure my body would not let me rest without a little help. Tears still slid down my cheeks as I lay on my pillow. My head pounded and a vision of Tim flashed over and over in my head. Soon darkness set in as sleep consumed my body and vanquished my thoughts.

Chapter 32
Praying For Wisdom

Again I awoke to the sound of tapping on my door.

"Annette?"

I lay quietly and still tired, I hoped whoever it was would just go away but the door squeaked as it slowly opened.

"Annette, you've got a phone call," Lynn whispered. "He called three times in the last two hours. I told him each time that you were sleeping but now he won't take no for an answer."

I peered up at her standing in the doorway.

"Thanks, Lynn," I said waving my hand. "I'll be right there."

As she closed the door, I yawned and slowly slid out of bed. I put on my robe, left my room and shuffled past the loud television in the living room. Jim and Zack were watching sports.

"Hey" they said in unison and I waved back at them as I headed for the phone in the kitchen.

"You look terrible," Zack noted and I facetiously stuck my tongue out at him.

"Hello?"

"Hi." It was Aaron's dreamy voice.

The struggle immediately began in my head and heart again. One of these men was bound to get hurt and I dreaded the thought.

"Want to get some dinner?" he asked, hopefulness evident in his voice.

"Not tonight, Aaron. You woke me up and I didn't get to sleep last night at work. I'm just worn out. How about a rain check?" I stood by the counter shifting from one foot to the other.

"Oh, can we get together tomorrow then?" he asked anxiously.

I knew I needed to talk with him but I also felt the need to understand my own head and heart. Then I made a decision; it was time to put an end to this internal struggle and make up my mind once and for all. But how would I ever do that when both Aaron and Tim meant so much to me?

"Sure," I conceded.

"You don't sound too excited about seeing me."

"I'm just tired, Aaron," I replied in a less than pleasant tone.

"Pick you up at ten?"

"Ten. Night, Aaron."

Lynn and Jessica sat at the kitchen table pretending to do their homework. When I got off the phone, they bombarded me with questions.

"Did I hear you say Aaron?" asked Lynn.

"Yes," I sighed. My head slumped down and I stared at the floor. As I turned to leave, Lynn piped up again.

"What about Tim?"

Tears filled my eyes and I rushed to my room - the two girls followed me. They plopped themselves on my bed, while I rustled under my covers and sat with my legs folded underneath.

"What is this about Aaron? Are you still engaged to Tim? When did Aaron come back? I thought you two were no longer an item anymore? Does Tim know that Aaron is around?"

Lynn and Jessica shot question after question so fast that I did not have time to even think. When I broke down sobbing, Lynn ran to the bathroom to grab some toilet paper to wipe my tears, while Jessica held me tight. They waited for me to calm down before demanding the whole sordid story.

I told them about the car accident, how I found out it was Aaron that I saved and showed them the torn letter from his dad. Lynn got some tape to put it back together so they both could read it. I also related how Aaron showed up at the beauty salon and the date we had.

"You didn't!" said Lynn with a look of disapproval.

Jessica glanced at Lynn and then turned to me. I closed my eyes and shook my head shamefully.

"What about Tim?" she asked. "Does he know?"

"Yes," I sighed. "I told him this morning."

Both girls kept their eyes glued on my face.

"Well?" they both said at once.

I started to choke on the tears at the back of my throat.

"He is so hurt. I didn't mean to do that. What's wrong with me?" I asked wiping tears away with my hands. "Maybe I shouldn't have said anything to him."

"You did the right thing," Lynn confirmed and looked down at my engagement ring.

"So who do you love?" asked Jessica.

Those words stung in my heart. I grabbed my sheets and wiped my face again.

"Both" I whispered.

"I think you should stay with Tim," offered Lynn moving behind me to rub my back. "After all, he was there for you when Aaron stopped writing." After a moment, she added, "Plus he helped you through school. You two have a lot in common. In fact, you even look like you belong together."

Memories again rushed in as I recalled the first time Tim kissed my cheek and how he slowly grew on me. It wasn't planned; it just happened. He held a flame for me until I was ready to take it and it was true that we both wanted the same things out of life.

"I think she should go back to Aaron," said Jessica putting in her two cents. "After all, he was her first love and no one ever forgets their first love. Besides, he was just thinking of you - being stuck with a cripple and all. He didn't want to put you out. I think that's so romantic."

Of course, Aaron then swept across my mind. My heart still fluttered when I heard his name. We only shared a few days before he left for the army but we wrote and when he was on leave, we escaped into each other's arms. I wondered what might have happened if he never stopped writing. Would Tim ever have had a chance?

Lynn sat up straight and glared at Jessica.

"How romantic is it to make her cry and think he didn't love her anymore," she noted clearly annoyed.

Jessica sprang to her knees, planted her hands firmly on her waist and stuck her face at Lynn.

"He only had her well being in mind," she said in a heated tone. "He didn't mean to hurt her. As a matter of fact, he tried to be thoughtful."

Lynn rose higher on her knees and pointed a finger at Jessica. "Can't you see how happy Annette has been since she became engaged to Tim?"

"Yeah, but I saw how happy she was when Aaron was around too," Jessica noted brushing Lynn's finger from her face.

"Do you remember her sulking after he quit writing," Lynn retorted.

Their arguing caused my head to pound and I rubbed my temples. I knew they meant well but this was not their decision.

"Okay, girls," I said flailing my arms in the air. "I don't need this right now." Both of them fell silent and sat back down on the bed.

How could this have happened? I wondered. Why is life – and love - so confusing?

"What are you going to do?" asked Lynn quietly.

I had heard all the pros and cons but knew there was more to it than that.

"I don't know yet. I really need to be alone so I can sort this out."

Jessica slipped off the bed and hugged me before leaving the room.

"Honey, I'm here if you need me," Lynn said getting up.

I looked at her and tried to smile. She leaned in and kissed me on the cheek before she left too. Without thinking I got down on my knees and prayed a small prayer for wisdom. More tears fell as I tried to sleep. I loved two men but needed to be true to myself. What did I want? After hiding under my pillow for a while so no one would hear me cry, I finally fell asleep.

When I awoke, I knew it would be the day of reckoning – I had to choose which person would cry and which would smile. It would be the hardest day of my life. I showered, dressed and sprayed on some perfume. Physically, I was ready. Mentally and emotionally, I was still unsure of my ultimate decision but it was not fair to leave either of them hanging. I recalled Tim so upset as he walked away angry and hurt but I also remembered Aaron, destroyed and damaged from all he'd been through. I waited for Aaron outside on the porch.

"Good morning, beautiful," he said leaning in to kiss me.

He looked so handsome with his black hair hanging down over the collar of his shirt. His tight polo shirt showed off his muscular shoulders and chest. It brought me back to the first time we met.

"Have you had breakfast yet?"

"No," I replied shaking my head. My heart fluttered in my chest as he put out his right arm. I slipped my hand around it and we strode to his car.

"Where to my lady?" he asked bowing before me.

"Anywhere," I chuckled.

He drove to the diner across from the hospital. When he parked the car, he would not let me open my door insisting that I wait for him. I handed him his crutch and he wobbled to the passenger door. Then he escorted me inside and the hostess found us a booth.

"How are you, Annette?" he asked in a serious voice.

"Good."

Aaron likely sensed the doubt in my tone but chose to ignore it. He said he visited the college the other day and signed up to go back to school. He took my advice and would learn to become a teacher. His college credits from a few years ago would be used toward his degree. At that moment, I realized we had grown apart. We had taken entirely different paths in our lives.

However, I listened intently as his words belied the excitement he felt. He'd finally figured out what he wanted to do with his life and I could not have been happier for him. I asked an occasional question now and then preferring to let him talk. He spoke of his past mission in the army and I sensed the disappointment he felt over his decision to join in the first place. I wondered if he'd still feel the same way if he had not lost his leg.

Either way, Aaron said he learned from me that no matter how impossible life might seem he had to pick himself up and go on. The grief might not go away completely but after a while, it would not feel so overwhelming. He reached across the table and squeezed my hand, his dark eyes searching mine.

"Remember the night we made love?" he asked.

"Yes, of course. That was the night I gave you all of me," I sighed aloud.

"Do you regret it?" he asked, his hand letting mine go.

"No," I said surprised and hurt. "That was my first time. I'll never forget that night and in its own way, it will always be special to me. What happened between us was beautiful."

The waitress arrived to take our order and I used the time to find the right words.

"I've been thinking where we would be now if you hadn't join the army."

"That would be my ring," he said, "and not someone else's."

Feeling uncomfortable, I dropped my hands into my lap. The past seemed to loom heavily over us, overwhelming in its intensity. For a brief moment, I wanted to hold Aaron in my arms to recapture everything we lost but the waitress interrupted again laying two glasses of water on the table.

"Does he know I'm around?" Aaron asked out of the blue. I could see the hurt on his face.

"Yes," I said swallowing hard.

"And?" he asked, bitterness overtaking his voice.

The waitress set down our plates and Aaron looked up to thank her. I picked up my fork and nervously poked a piece of melon. Aaron scooped up some eggs and rolled them into his mouth. It was my turn to talk but I was not sure how to proceed. However, I knew this was no time to chicken out. It would not be fair to Aaron or Tim. My body stiffened and my mouth formed a tight line.

"This is goodbye, Aaron," I said finally.

"I don't understand," he replied, disappointment written all over his face.

"Yes, I think you do," I said. "I'm getting married." I let that sink in for a moment and summonsed the strength to impart what I needed to say next.

"He's a good man, Aaron… and even though I love you, I'm not willing to lose what I have with him. We grew a strong bond of love together after you left me and he was there for me."

We sat in the diner silently staring at our plates without finishing our meals. Suddenly, I felt nauseated.

"Ready to go home then?" he asked finally.

"Yes," I responded, a single tear sliding down my face.

At the car Aaron offered a sad smile as he opened my door. No more words were spoken on the way home until we reached my house.

"I love you, Annette and I always will," he breathed as tears rolled down his face. "You were the best thing that ever happened to me. You made me feel alive again and I want you to know that you are the very best part of me. I'll never forget you."

He leaned in and kissed me on the lips before taking me in his arms and holding me tight. We stayed that way for a while and when we finally separated, I knew this would be the last time I would ever hold him. After I left the car and walked to the curb, his eyes found mine.

"I really do love you, Annette."

"Goodbye, Aaron" I softly replied.

I knew there was no easy way to say those words without them cutting into his heart but it was something I

could no longer avoid. Even thought part of me wanted to race back to him, I just could not do it. I had finally made my decision and truly believed it was the right one for me. As I entered the house, I could not help feeling a little lighter – as if a huge weight had been lifted - and I smiled as I considered my future with Tim. The only thing that could destroy that dream was if he could not forgive me and refused to take me back. I shuddered at the thought.

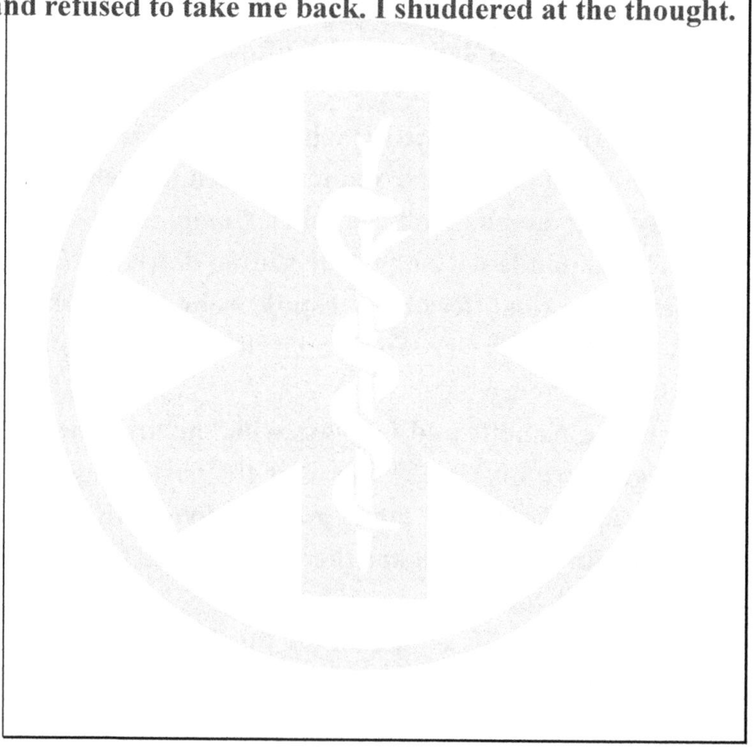

Chapter 33
The Right Decision

I settled back on my bed, a cloud of depression hanging ominously over me. I realized that I must be crazy to break up with one man without even knowing whether the other man still loved me. Yes, I cared deeply for Aaron. He was a wonderful part of my past, someone I would never forget. Tim on the other hand, I grew to love with all my heart and soul. I truly believed that he was meant to be my future. I withdrew the essence of my heart from Aaron and gave it to Tim. Not only was he a gentle, kind and loving human being, he also made me laugh. I prayed that he still wanted me.

For a while, I paced my room with nervous anxiety. I had to go to him, face him and stare into his eyes. It could not wait. I needed to know if he still loved me. I gazed at my engagement ring remembering the day he proposed and came up with a plan. Quickly, I ran to my car making my first stop our Chinese restaurant. Tim was working all day so I swung by the firehouse. Luckily, the fire truck was parked in the garage. I caught my breath and got out of my car holding a bag of goodies in my hand.

"Hey," a few fellows said when I entered.

Then I saw Tim, his face drawn, sad and frowning.

"Hey," I ventured with a slight smile.

He shifted awkwardly on his feet and then glanced at my hand to see if I was still wearing his ring. A small smile appeared but just as fast, it disappeared.

"Hey," he replied gloomily.

I walked over and kissed him on the cheek. Can he tell how scared I am? I wondered.

Tim did not move so I reached for his hand and squeezed his fingers. He squeezed back giving me some kind of response and a surge of warmth filled my heart. Just the sensation of his touch seemed to reaffirm our love and I knew I made the right decision - but was it too late?

"Come on. Follow me," I coaxed pulling his arm.

All of the pent-up emotion of the day burst to the surface and I squeezed my eyes closed to stop the tears. I was frightened, anxious and happy all at the same time.

"Where are we going?" he asked dryly, his eyes studying me. He looked like he had aged with lines under his eyes from lack of sleep.

"Trust me, please," I urged pressing my lips together.

Reluctantly, he asked to hold my bag and followed me to the park. We walked in silence beside each other and reaching a bench near the playground, we sat down. We could hear a few children laughing as they slid happily down the slide.

Sometimes the hardest thing to do is be humble. I owed him a huge apology and did not expect him to forgive me. I only hoped that he would. I cleared my throat stalling for another minute while Tim sat motionless and stared straight ahead.

"I'm so sorry," I murmured and squeezed his arm.

"I am too," he replied glumly. I could not interpret his words. Was he happy I was there or did he hate me? We sat again in awkward silence. I hated the insecure feeling

in the air around us. It felt so wrong, especially after everything we had been through. With each passing moment, I grew even more afraid that he would reject me but I knew it was a chance I had to take. I had a plan and finally mustered the courage to see it through.

"Are you hungry?" I asked. "It's around lunch time and I brought us food from our favorite restaurant."

"I haven't had much of an appetite," he shrugged.

I opened the package and tried to pass him some food but he would not take it.

"Why are you really here, Annette?" His blue eyes searched my face for an answer.

"I really needed to see you," I confessed as I tucked a piece of hair behind my ear.

I knew that was not the answer he wanted to hear. In the distance, a child fell off a swing and his mother ran over to soothe his cries.

"Here," I said taking cookies from the bag and placing one in his hand.

Tim gave me an odd glance.

"I'll open mine first," I said trying to be optimistic. I broke the cookie open and took out the fortune. "Life isn't always fair," I read aloud.

His eyebrows turned down over his nose. Perhaps he was afraid of what his fortune might say.

"Now it's your turn," I said knowing he did not really want to play this game. "Humor me. Please, Timothy." I pleaded.

He quickly looked up at me because I never called him that before, using his whole first name. Breaking the cookie in half, he slid out the paper and read its contents.

"I still want to be your wife if you will have me," he said with no emotion.

Then I bent down on my knees holding out my hands to him. Obviously startled, he glanced down at me. A single tear accidentally slipped down my cheek.

"So what does this mean?" he asked. "Have you made up your mind?"

That was not quite the response I had hoped for or expected.

"Yes."

"And what about Aaron?" he asked, his body beginning to shake.

"He will always be special to me, Tim. He was my first love but we drifted apart." I waited quietly for a moment to let him take in what I said. "Then you came along. Even though I tried to fight my feelings, you were always at my side – always open and willing to comfort me. Now I am hopelessly in love with you, Tim."

His eyes squinted from the bright sun shining overhead and I watched his face as he considered my words.

"Will you still have me?" I asked weakly still on my knees. "I love you so much."

Tim leaned down and wiped the tear from my cheek. It was then that I noticed he was crying too.

"I could never turn you away, Annette. I love you and always will," he said lifting me up.

He took me in his arms and gently kissed my lips. Then I buried my face in his shoulder as he held me.

"You have made me the happiest man in the world," he whispered.

Epilogue

The date is April 19, 2000, exactly five years after the Oklahoma bombing. Excitement permeates the air as President Clinton arrives to dedicate a memorial built for the men, women and children who lost their lives that awful day.

The memorial is beautiful with a reflecting pool flanked by two large gates, and a field of symbolic bronze and stone chairs – one for each person lost, arranged according to what floor of the building they were on at the time of the blast. The seats of the children are smaller than those of the adults. Also part of the memorial is a chain link fence that has attracted countless personal items like cards, teddy bears and pictures.

When I think back to that fateful day, I wonder how mixing ammonium nitrate/fuel oil and nitro methane can create such a highly explosive bomb. I actually lived through that time in Oklahoma's history and it still hurts deeply to know that an American militia movement sympathizer created that deadly bomb. By the time the dust cleared, many people lost their lives or were injured.

Tim had related his father's experience that day. When his fire truck pulled up to the disaster, the firefighters' could feel their adrenalin rising but had to cage their fear and anger, holding only onto hope. They quickly realized that one-third of the building was blown away leaving smoke, debris and fire all around the streets. Bodies' lay everywhere - some so mangled that they could not be identified.

He related how the smoke-filled air felt suffocating, which made it difficult for the firefighters to breath. Their view of the site was also distorted. Many people were trapped and in the distance, they could hear their screams. If their job was not dangerous enough, hearing their cries made it almost unbearable.

His father told him that it really did look like the end of the world and even days later, the stench of the dead still in the remains of the building filled the air. It took weeks to clear out the rubble and rebuild the city. Many people were deeply affected by this bombing, even those far from the scene. Mothers and fathers lost children. Men lost their wives and women lost their husbands.

Some people prayed to God thanking him for allowing them to arrive late for work that morning or for calling in sick. At the time, this blast was the deadliest domestic attack in United States history and it changed the way we live in the United States today.

There are now glass barriers surrounding many offices and federal buildings. Heavily armed security forces routinely patrol train stations and airports.

The memorial sight means a great deal to both of us. I can't help crying as I recall that horrible day, which changed our lives forever. This unbelievable act of violence led me to begin paramedic school where I met Tim. Over time, we learned that we held similar values and the same goal in life - to help others. And in a strange and unpredictable way, this incident also helped me find true love. Tim and I have now been married for two years and I am pregnant with our first child.

As we stand holding hands in the bright sunshine with hundreds of others listening to the president, I see a familiar figure in one corner by the fence. He has a crutch and is missing part of his left leg. I am pretty sure I know who it is but have not seen or talked to him over the last few years. I will always remember Aaron but my heart belongs to Tim and the new family we have planned together.

Life is funny, isn't it? One event leads right into another and at times, we're not quite sure where our path will take us. But in the end although we will never fully understand, it all seems part of a much grander design. As we see our life's plan unfold, we realize that God knows what is best for us after all.

Made in the USA
Middletown, DE
03 November 2022